KU-469-547

Mad Dogs & Scotsmen

Gerald Hammond

WARWICKSHIRE
COUNTY LIBRARY

CONTROL No.

FIC

G.K. Hall & Co. • Chivers Press
Thorndike, Maine USA   Bath, Avon, England

This Large Print edition is published by G.K. Hall & Co., USA and by Chivers Press, England.

Published in 1996 in the U.S. by arrangement with St. Martin's Press, Inc.

Published in 1997 in the U.K. by arrangement with Macmillan General Books Ltd.

U.S.   Softcover   0-7838-1890-4 (Paperback Collection Edition)
U.K.   Hardcover   0-7451-6976-7 (Chivers Large Print)
U.K.   Softcover   0-7451-6978-3 (Camden Large Print)

Copyright © Gerald Hammond 1995

The right of Gerald Hammond to be identified as the author of this work has been asserted by him in accordance with the Copyright, Designs and Patents Act 1988.

All rights reserved.

The text of this Large Print edition is unabridged.
Other aspects of the book may vary from the original edition.

Set in 16 pt. Bookman Old Style by Minnie B. Raven.

Printed in the United States on permanent paper.

British Library Cataloguing in Publication Data available

Library of Congress Cataloging in Publication Data

Hammond, Gerald, 1926–
    Mad dogs & Scotsmen / Gerald Hammond.
       p.   cm.
    ISBN 0-7838-1890-4 (lg. print : sc)
    1. Large type books.   I. Title.
    [PR6058.A55456M3   1996b]
    823'.914—dc20   96-25010

We hope you have enjoyed this Large Print book. Other G.K. Hall & Co. or Chivers Press Large Print books are available at your library or directly from the publishers.

For more information about current and upcoming titles, please call or write, without obligation, to:

G.K. Hall & Co.
P.O. Box 159
Thorndike, Maine 04986
USA
Tel. (800) 223-2336

OR

Chivers Press Limited
Windsor Bridge Road
Bath BA2 3AX
England
Tel. (0225) 335336

All our Large Print titles are designed for easy reading, and all our books are made to last.

I have to thank Barbara Whitehead and her friend Dr Galbraith for their technical help.

I would also like to make it clear that any individual or firm mentioned in this book is totally fictitious, and no resemblance to any real-life counterpart is intended.

G.H.

Preface

Daffy shook her hair with its spangled stripe running through it, and the fine chain which linked her ear to her right nostril glinted in the spring sunshine. That day's kit featured a black leather jacket over a transparent miniskirt and not very much beneath. 'No sweat,' she said. 'Go for it.'

Hannah looked at Daffy as if at some strange animal. She had never quite got used to her colleague's manner or style of dress. Hannah wore her usual uniform of a neat blouse and jeans. 'I'm sure we can manage,' she said primly.

From the first, I had tried to set my face against taking in boarders. We were, I said many times, a breeding and training kennels. Our stock and trainees were with us for months at least. And we knew about working spaniels. Short-stay boarders would include rare breeds with rare troubles and they would spread their infections to each other and, much worse, to our precious residents. And what about cats?

My voice might just as well have been crying in some damn wilderness. My two partners were of a single mind and it was made up.

Beth, my wife, insisted that the holiday visitors need never mix with the residents and pupils in training. And cats could be turned away.

Isobel, my other partner, her spectacles flashing indignantly, pointed out, first, that she was a qualified vet and perfectly capable of dealing with whatever arose; second, that nowadays inoculation could protect against almost anything short of old age and we already insisted on the production of certificates; and, third, that since circumstances had tricked us into employing two simultaneous, full-time kennel-maids we had better justify their wages by expanding the business.

Without going so far as to admit that I was wrong, I bowed to their combined wills. The isolation kennels, originally built to accommodate infectious stock or occasional bitches in season, were extended, visitors were accepted and to my surprise the venture proved profitable enough to meet the wages bill with a little to spare. Dogs boarded while their owners snatched a holiday abroad were far less demanding of our time than young pups or older dogs left for training for the shooting field.

The next step on the road away from our chosen specialization was taken when a nearby quarantine kennels lost its authorization from the Department of Agriculture and Fisheries, for breaches of the Acts of 1974 and 1981 (as amended) flagrant enough to ensure that they would never get it back. Pressure was on, not only from my partners and staff but also from dog-owners and even, in an oblique way, from the Scottish Office, for us to fill the gap.

The two kennel-maids, Daffy and Hannah, were in agreement for once and seemed more than willing to absorb the extra work, perhaps for fear that redundancy would otherwise claim one or even both of them. Daffy had left us a year earlier to get married but she had been so good at the job, despite eccentricity bordering on the completely zany, that when Rex, her husband, found work on the oil-rigs and Daffy, finding time heavy on her hands, wanted her old job back, we agreed instantly. The trouble was that during her absence we had employed Hannah. And Hannah, who had been engaged on a temporary basis to oblige her father, had settled in well.

It happened that the stone walls of what had been byres when Three Oaks was a farm were still in good order although the roofs had gone, and these walls formed an ideal basis for a compound enclosing a group of kennels and runs. The work was

9

pushed through and Departmental hands were laid on it in blessing. Our position was ideal, near Leuchars Airbase and not far from Dundee Airport or the harbours on the Tay and the Forth. Word must have passed around, especially among servicemen returning from NATO postings with beloved dogs in hand. I had thought that they might be deterred by the considerable cost of keeping a dog in quarantine kennels for six months but I had underestimated the love of the average Brit for his mutt. Almost immediately, we were in danger of being overbooked.

The extra money, I had to admit, was welcome. Our income from breeding and training spaniels tended to be seasonal and I was comforted when, for the first time, we contrived not to dip into the red during the slack season. The dogs in quarantine might require feeding and general maintenance but so far from wasting precious time walking them, we were actually forbidden to do so. My associates absorbed the extra work without apparent effort and I was free to follow my main avocation as principal spaniel trainer and all-round worrier.

Everything in what had once been a garden before the puppies took it over seemed to be lovely. I began to relax, which may have been where I made my mistake. Sometimes I wonder whether, in my moments of worrying, I may not be fending off calamity by sheer willpower. Whenever I relax, disaster strikes.

One

At the time of the year which is sand-wiched between the winter sports and summer holiday seasons, when children and students are beginning the run-up to exams, holiday boarders were compara-tively few but most of our quarantine ken-nels were occupied. I remember among others the weird-looking and elderly mon-grel of an RAF corporal newly returned from the Middle East and also a pair of Weima-raners belonging to a couple whose habit it was to spend spring and summer at their hotel in Britain, returning to another hotel which they owned in South Africa for the spring and summer there. Their owners hoped to breed from the Weimaraners; I would have preferred to breed from the owners, who were by far our most remu-nerative clients.

Another regular visitor present at the time was a Bedlington, the pet and guard dog of an oil industry scientist who spent much of his time on contracts almost anywhere in the world, taking his dog with him but leaving the dog in quarantine with us during his occasional breaks at home.

And then there was Jove, for whom I had a special affection. Jove was a male black Labrador, solid rather than large in build, with a perfect head and a coat as glossy as an oiled gunstock. Jove had been through my hands several times before. His owner, who was in search of the perfect all-round sporting companion and coming very close to success, had sensibly left him with me for training in obedience and the basics of deer work. After a season of stalking, which had reinforced Jove's ability to point deer, follow up a heart-shot quarry and indicate the carcass, he had been returned to me to be trained for game-shooting. He had ended up as an expensive but valuable dog, a rarity who was adept at both jobs and a looker as well. I had heard on the grapevine that Jove's owner, Noel Cochrane, had turned down some substantial offers for him.

Jove had returned to me yet again after Cochrane had spent a year in India. Jove, whose owner had made a career in the field of animal immunization, had been vaccinated against rabies and every other canine malady known to man or dog; but the law was the law and exceptions were only made for valuable breeding stock going about their procreative business. On his return to Britain, into quarantine Jove came. I was pleased to have him back. He was a happy dog, secure and well balanced, rather puzzled by his sudden incarceration and saddened by the separation from his beloved owner, but he had confidence in the future. He knew that the good times would come again some day. Meanwhile, he was prepared to wait with the patience peculiar to Labradors and few other breeds.

I tried never to become too attached to my charges, but Jove was an exception. He had the kind of charm possessed by some dogs and few people. When things got on top of me, as they could easily do in the years following the illness which had once nearly killed me, I tried to spare Beth the burden of a husband's irrational depressions. Instead, I would go out and talk to Jove and he would look wise and talk back to me, very articulately considering his limitations, and so we would give each other comfort. He drew additional comfort from his favourite toy, a red rubber kangaroo. I always find it endearing when a Labrador, that most mature and dignified of breeds on the surface, reveals the puppyishness which is never far beneath.

We usually discouraged visits from owners as they tended to unsettle the long-stay residents, but Jove seemed to be reassured rather than unsettled by visits from Noel Cochrane and to accept philosophically that the time was not yet ripe for them to leave together. So I was not too surprised when, on my return from the set-aside land which had conveniently been established just over our boundary, I met Noel near the corner of the house. He was carrying a flat attaché case.

I sat the dogs and waited for him.

Noel knew quite a lot about my training methods by then, so I could trust him not to irritate me with humorous remarks. I had with me two springers still in an early stage of training and I was carrying, as I often do, a racket and a net of tennis balls. Several balls fired out into light cover could be hunted for by a dog with the virtual certainty of a quick success. (Only when the dog has learned to hunt and to obey easy hand signals do I move on to using a single, heavier dummy.) Some visitors had been known to enquire whether I was preparing for Wimbledon and were later quite properly surprised when our final accounting produced a figure far higher than they had expected. If a client wishes to poke fun at me, he is welcome to do so but he will pay for the privilege. The tariff is secret but quite clear in my mind.

Noel had always seemed to me to be built out of cubes, like some educational toy. He was thick-set. His thatch of curly brown hair, now greying, was set on a square head

on square shoulders. His legs, if not themselves square were sturdy. Strong jawbones
made his face into the squarest feature of
all, on which his habitually anxious expression looked out of place. That day, he
looked more harassed than anxious.

After the barest greeting, he said, 'Mrs
Kitts is making up my account. I've come
to fetch Jove.'

Noel was usually polite and friendly, even
a chatterbox. I could only guess that he was
in a hurry. 'You can't have him,' I said. 'I'm
not allowed to release a dog that's not long
back from India and half-way through its
quarantine period, no matter how loving the
owner.'

'I'm going abroad again.'

That was at least a little bit different.
'Hang on a minute while I kennel these two,'
I said.

'I'll come with you, if I may. Listen, John,
I'm being sent abroad again, probably for
good.'

'Where is it this time?' I asked.

'The States. California.'

'Lucky old you!'

'Sure. Smog, riots, fires, floods, landslides
and earthquakes. The playground of the
western world. Somebody went down with
a heart attack and they want me out there
for a course that starts in two days, so I
can't hang around.'

That at least explained a certain jumpiness in his manner. 'Jove could be sent on after you,' I pointed out.

'And stand a risk of being left over a whole weekend in some warehouse without food or water? Unless a courier was sent with him, and you know what that costs.'

That was slightly unfair. I could have put him in touch with several very reliable firms specializing in animal transport. On the other hand, allaying the anxiety of the owner is an important part of the service. I ushered the two dogs into the kennel they shared, closed the door of the run and we set off back towards the house.

'You've got . . . ?' There was a pause while I searched my memory. 'Certificate ID Fourteen stroke BM Four A?' I finished uncertainly. Isobel has a better memory for the tedious details of bureaucracy.

'Yes.' He dug it out of his pocket and showed it to me without slowing down.

'Even so, the next hurdle is that you have to have approved transport. Don't blame me, it's the rules. Owners have been known to let Fido out for walkies between the kennels and the ship.'

'I expected that. So I came out from Dundee by cab. I have a taxi plane waiting at Dundee. Can you take me to meet it? I'll pay, of course.'

I examined the certificate while still walking and nearly fell over a wheelbarrow. The certificate was in order. 'Do you have a travelling box for him?' I asked.

'I'll buy one off you,' he said quickly.

The rush of business was making up for my disappointment at losing Jove. I met Daffy coming out of the house. The stripe in her hair was green that day, I remember, to tone in with the fringed smock she was wearing, which seemed to have been home-made out of the discarded cloth from a snooker table. 'Get one of the larger travelling boxes,' I told her. 'Put in a fitted cushion . . .' I raised my eyebrows at Noel, who nodded impatiently. 'Back the car round to the quarantine kennels, put the big crate inside and the travelling box in the crate. You know the drill.'

She put on a patient expression, calculated to annoy me. 'I know it all except which dog I put in the box. Not Jove, leaving us?'

'I'm afraid so.' I gave her the keys to my old car. 'Load him up . . . along with Mr Cochrane's case. Unless your money's in it, Noel?'

He shook his head, hesitated and meekly handed over his attaché case.

'If Jove's travelling with you and you're going far,' Daffy said to Noel, 'you'll need a bowl for feed and water.' Noel nodded. 'Shall

I make up a package of dried dog-food to take with you?'

'Please.'

Daffy nodded and looked pleased as she bustled away. The well-being of the animals was far more important to her than the satisfaction of the customer or the profitability of the business.

'I know they're a pest, these quarantine regulations,' I said sympathetically as we continued towards the house. 'It's extra money for us, but I can recognize it's a bloody nuisance — even if I am laughing all the way to the bank. Other countries can't follow the same system because they aren't islands, yet they seem to manage. Pets are vaccinated, they scatter medicated bait laced with the same sort of preparation for foxes or whatever happens to be the local vector of rabies, and if you get bitten you go for injections damn quick. That's how it's done. The presence of rabies doesn't even make much impact on their lives. And I read somewhere that of all the cases of rabies in humans during the last fifteen years or so, only two were contracted in Europe. But, of course, you know all that,' I added. 'It's your field.'

He grunted. 'Rabies isn't something to mess with,' he said. 'It's an appalling death when it does happen, and once the symptoms show up it's too late to do much about it.'

'Maybe. I don't mind being paid to house the dogs, but word in the trade is that of the eighty or so quarantine kennels in the country the vast majority have never seen a case of rabies, so how do we justify the cost and nuisance value that we put on holiday-makers and working-dog enthusiasts? But they're going to have to change their tune. If rabies isn't exterminated on the Continent, there'll soon be a risk of it finding its way through the Channel Tunnel. Either way, we'll have to go over to the Continental system. Will that hurt your business?'

'It'll do it a world of good. How about yours?'

'We survived before we ever became a quarantine kennels,' I said as we arrived at the house door, 'and I dare say we can do so again.'

I took Noel indoors. We had long since outgrown the original tiny office and had turned over what had once been Daffy's bedroom for the purpose. Hannah was now accommodated in a temporary building beside the barn, pending the construction of more permanent housing. (Daffy had a room in her grandmother's house in the village which, now that they were properly married, Rex was allowed to share when he was ashore.) One snag to the present layout was that visitors to the office had to pass

20

through the kitchen. Such are the penalties of converting an old farmhouse instead of building from scratch.

I paused by the stove to offer Noel coffee from the eternal supply percolating there but he shook his head. 'I'll be awash with coffee by the time I touch down at LA,' he said.

Isobel was in the office, making out Noel's account. She looked at us seriously through her pink-framed spectacles. Isobel usually looks like any middle-class, middle-aged housewife with no worries or ambitions beyond tomorrow's dinner and next year's holiday, but in fact she is a qualified vet and an inspired handler of dogs in the field trials which form such a vital shop-window for our trained spaniels.

Noel's account was already substantial. To it, we added the cost of the travelling box and cushion and a feeding bowl. The package of meal and the trip to Dundee I threw in out of the goodness of my heart.

'Is my cheque good enough?' Noel asked.

I was about to say that of course it was, but Isobel, the hard-headed member of the firm, got in first. 'Not if you're going abroad for a long period,' she said. 'Altogether too much trouble sorting it out if there are any queries.' She meant if it bounced but was too polite to say the words aloud. 'Don't you have traveller's cheques?'

'Well, yes,' Noel said stiffly. He pulled out a folder, started signing. Traveller's cheques, in my experience, usually arrive with the largest denominations at the back. On that assumption and judging from the thickness of the wad, he was carrying a very large sum on him.

Daffy put her head in. 'Car's back at the front door with Jove inside,' she said. 'I'll miss the old bugger. Mr Cochrane's case is in the cubby-hole under the floor at the back.'

'Thank you.' Noel hesitated and then took out his wallet. Daffy came all the way into the room and a crisp note changed hands. Daffy raised her eyebrows. 'Thanks a bunch,' she said, 'but this is in dollars.'

'I can change it for you,' I said. I still go to the States occasionally and I keep a small reserve of dollars handy rather than pay the bank a commission every time I change money to and fro.

'Thanks again,' Daffy said with more genuine warmth and withdrew into the kitchen.

Isobel produced a buff envelope. 'Jove's immunization certificates,' she said. 'His Form ID Seventy. And his pedigree. You left it with us, remember? And there's a receipt in there.'

'Great!' Noel shook Isobel's hand and turned about. In the kitchen, Beth was now busily preparing lunch while Sam, our son, stood holding on to the side of his playpen and gave a running commentary on his mother's activities which would have been of great interest if only somebody other than Beth had been able to understand it.

Noel exchanged a polite but hasty word of farewell with Beth and then followed me through the hall and out to the front. I had my hand out to open the car door when I froze.

The spread of gravel and the drive beyond were empty.

I heard Noel draw in his breath.

Upstairs, the bathroom toilet flushed and a moment later Daffy came pattering downstairs. She had something red in her hand. 'Hold on a moment,' she called and came to the door.

'Where's the car?' I asked her.

She moved all the way outside and looked around. Her face fell. 'It was right here five minutes ago,' she said. 'Looks like some bugger's swiped it.' She opened her hand and showed us the rubber kangaroo. 'Jove'll be lost without this,' she said disconsolately.

I stood there for several seconds, looking and feeling stupid. In my ordered life, cars did not simply vanish. My face must have shown some of the tumult in my mind.

23

'Losing the car isn't the end of the world,' Daffy said, offering what comfort she could. 'Cool down. It's insured, isn't it?'

I nodded. I had sent off the cheque only the previous month.

'There you are then. That old banger didn't owe you anything. Quite the reverse. It was on about its third trip round the clock and only held together by rust. High time we had a new one.'

She was exaggerating, of course, but there was something in what she said. I had other worries.

Beth had come to the door and heard us. 'But what about Jove?' she asked. 'He's a valuable dog.'

Noel had lost his colour. For a moment I knew what he would look like in twenty years' time. 'He's a lot more than money on the hoof,' he said shakily. 'He's Jove. And he's not insured. They wouldn't cover him in India and there didn't seem to be any need while he was here.'

Beth was missing the point. 'He was also in quarantine,' I reminded her. I glanced at Noel again. As I watched, he went from white to red. I thought that he might faint. 'We'll get him back,' I said.

'My briefcase,' Noel said in a voice that was hardly more than a whisper.

'I'll tell you something else,' Daffy said to me. For a usually extrovert girl she sounded defensive. 'Your gun's in the car. I moved it to under the back seat because Mr Cochrane's briefcase was just the right size for the cubbyhole under the floor at the back. You're always telling me not to leave guns and things on view. It's all right,' she added quickly. 'It was Old Faithful, not your new one.'

'And it didn't occur to you that I'd have to heave the crate out before I could give Mr Cochrane his case?' I asked reproachfully.

'That's no longer much of a point,' Noel said.

My mind had been trying to swim in treacle while digesting too many new thoughts all at once. His last words brought me to my senses. I turned back into the house. 'Got to call the police,' I said.

'Let's think about that,' Noel said.

'Nothing to think about,' I retorted. 'We have a stolen car which may be heading for a smash — or a bank robbery. A stolen shotgun which could also be on its way to a bank hold-up. And we have a stolen dog which was in quarantine. You know and I know that he had been thoroughly proofed against rabies, but the law doesn't take that into account. The last two alone demand that the police be told, forthwith if not sooner, plus several other authorities. After that, we're required to run round in small circles, wringing our hands and whimpering. The law's quite clear on the subject.'

'If you can joke . . .' Beth began.

'Gallows humour,' I told her.

'You're sure we must call the cops immediately?' Beth asked me. 'There's going to be an awful fuss. Run down to the gate,' she told Daffy. 'Just in case somebody's made a mistake or playing a joke or something.'

'Right.' Daffy vanished.

We were back in the kitchen by then and Isobel had come out of the office in time to hear some of what was said and guess the rest. 'Of course John's right,' she said. 'If we don't call the police in straight away it could make everything thirty times worse.'

I decided that an emergency call would get action started a little earlier if only by a second or two. I keyed nine-nine-nine and asked for the police. As I was connected Daffy showed up in the door and shook her head. She joined the others who were leaning against the table or the fitments, too nervous to sit down — except, that is, for Beth, who was crouched by the playpen. Sam himself had curled up for a nap on the rug. I felt a momentary pang at the picture of mother and child. Beth looks so young, although she is remarkably tough and resilient, and it came to me for the thousandth time that I was responsible for these two beings. Any threat to me threatened them.

I reported the theft of my car, very reluctantly adding the information that the car contained a shotgun and a dog in quarantine. The voice on the other end, sounding scandalized, promised that all cars would be warned of the theft and that officers would call on us soon for a statement. I raised my eyebrows at Noel but he shook his head violently. The call finished and I hung up.

'You don't want anything said about your briefcase?' I asked Noel.

'Not at this stage,' he said. I waited, but he volunteered nothing more.

I had been standing at the wall-mounted phone in the kitchen. Isobel pushed me gently into one of the basket chairs and took the phone. 'Rest yourself,' she said. 'I'll phone Henry.'

'Why Henry? We've got to notify the local authority and the Department.'

'At least Henry still has a car, which is more than you do. We may need transport before you get your car back. If you ever do. Of course, there's a silver lining,' she said with an attempt at cheerfulness. 'As far as the car's concerned, you may be better off if it never turns up. It's overdue for replacement and we could use the tax write-off.'

This was so close to what Daffy had said that involuntarily I glanced around, but Daffy was still absent.

Sam woke up and began to talk. Beth, readily interpreting his private language, got up to prepare his evening meal so I gathered that he was complaining of hunger.

Noel detached himself from the big table and came to stand over me. 'Do you have to mention me by name?' he asked. 'Where I am and where I'm going are supposed to be deep commercial secrets at the moment. Couldn't you just do your best to recover Jove on behalf of "a client"? No,' he added quickly, 'of course you couldn't. Pay no attention to my idiot ramblings. You'll have to explain what Jove was doing outside the secure area.'

'Is there anything valuable in your case?' I asked him.

'Not intrinsically valuable. Just papers.' For a moment he looked as though he was going to explain. Then he rubbed his head of curly hair and said, 'Important is something else.'

I wanted to ask him what he meant but decided that he would be unlikely to tell me. And I would probably find out anyway. When the pot gets stirred, the first things to float to the surface are secrets. All the same, it seemed to me that Noel was even more nervous than I was and more so than even the absence of Jove could explain.

Isobel hung up the phone. 'Henry's coming over,' she said.

I was pleased. I even began to relax slightly. Isobel's elderly husband is a sure source of calm, sound advice.

Stemming from a so-called rationalization of police resources, the local police station was no longer permanently manned, but the Constable who still lived in the village must have been somewhere in the neighbourhood because he managed to dead-heat with Henry, who had had only a couple of miles to drive and must have left within seconds of Isobel's phone call.

We had not had much to do with this constable since his predecessor — who had become as close to a friend as discipline allowed — had been promoted and moved to Kirkcaldy. The replacement was older than the usual run of baby-faced constables. He was evidently a man who had missed promotion and was coasting towards retirement, but in my few dealings with him I had found him patient, thorough and polite. He was tall and well-built but with the beginnings of a belly on him. His was the flat-backed head common in northeast Scotland. His hair was greying, but the day was marching on and his jaw was beginning to show blue.

Henry took a seat in one of the Windsor chairs but the Constable — Constable Buchan, I remembered suddenly — took a stand in front of the unlit Aga and handy to the wall-phone. His first act was to use the radio clipped to his tunic to report his arrival and to relay our phone number to his Control.

'It's better not to use the radio when it's unnecessary,' he told us apologetically. 'Thieves ken fine how to listen in. And we're getting awfu' short of wavelengths. Now, tell me what's adae.' He opened his incident book on the mantelpiece.

I recounted the story, speaking as much to Henry as to Constable Buchan. I introduced Noel and referred to him as 'a client' but Buchan insisted on his name and wrote it down with the others, carefully checking the spelling of all our names.

When I came to the contents of the car, he looked solemn. 'These are serious matters,' he said. 'The proper authorities are being informed about the dog. But, man alive, what possessed you to leave a gun in an unlocked car?'

I decided that I might as well get in a little practice at answering a question which was bound to be asked over and over again in the coming days. 'I was about to take several dogs away in the car for steadiness training on rabbits,' I explained, 'so I put the gun into its hidden compartment and locked the car. Then one of the kennel-maids asked me to deal first with two younger dogs so that she could clean their run, turn their bedding and so on. So I spent a few minutes with them over in the field. Then Mr Cochrane showed up and I told the other kennel-maid to load his dog and his case. She transferred the gun to below the back seat to make room for the case in the under-floor compartment and she left the car at the door ready for me to drive away.' A potentially useful lie occurred to me. 'When I went out a minute or two later, I intended to take the gun out and lock it away, but the car was gone.'

The Constable decided not to read me a lecture but to leave it to those whose job it was to pontificate on firearms security. 'Well,' he said, 'no doubt the lads from Firearms will be wanting a chat with you about it.'

'No doubt,' I said. I could see endless trouble and quite possibly a revoking of my shotgun certificate. I would get it back in the end — the courts are never as arbitrary as the police in such matters — but in the meantime our training activities would be hampered. Fortunately, Beth and Isobel had their own certificates, to facilitate compliance with the law if I should be ill or abroad.

'What was the serial number of the missing gun?'

I would have had to go and consult my certificate or my insurance policy but Beth, who regularly amazes me by showing a foresight appropriate to someone far more mature than her very youthful appearance suggests, had already looked it up.

Daffy had returned with Hannah. I thought that they were holding hands, which surprised me because the two had never even pretended to like each other. Then I saw that Daffy was dragging the other girl by the wrist.

'You'd better hear what Hannah saw,' Daffy said. Evidently feeling that she had done all that was required of her, she approached the stove and seemed to lose interest.

Hannah had not needed to be dragged forward. She was eager to make her contribution. 'I was Hoovering the grass,' she began.

The Constable, who had blinked in amazement or disbelief at Daffy, had then looked on Hannah's conventional, blonde prettiness with approval, but I could see that he was now beginning to have his doubts about her. 'I beg your pardon, Miss?' he said.

'That's quite right,' I explained. 'We've just got a new machine, a sort of vacuum cleaner, to lift dog-plonks and other litter off the grass.'

'Have you now? I shall have to see this some time. Go on, Miss.'

'I was Hoovering the lawn,' Hannah repeated firmly. 'The machine isn't all that quiet, in fact it sounds a bit like a jumbo jet calling to its mate, so I didn't hear anything. But I looked up whenever my attention was attracted by movement, seen out of the corner of my eye.'

'You saw the car taken?' asked the Constable quickly.

'Not exactly,' Hannah said. I think that we all slumped slightly in disappointment. 'But I think that I saw the person who took it,' she added. We all perked up again. 'I saw somebody walk up the drive. I thought they went to the front door. Not more than half a minute later, I looked up again and the car was going down the drive and out of the gate. It drove straight on, it didn't turn right for the village.'

'But you did not see the man in the driving seat?' Buchan asked.

'No. And it wasn't a man. It was a woman.'

'Are you sure?' I said. It was a stupid question, but theft of cars and guns had seemed much more likely to be a man's crime than a woman's. I began to revise my ideas. If the target had been the dog, the Animal Rights activists might be behind it, and the sincerest members of that lunatic fringe are predominantly female. Not that that put a more cheerful complexion on things. Animal Rights fanatics could be just as ruthless as any other criminal and, strangely, seemed to have no compunction about themselves killing or maiming animals.

Hannah smiled patiently. 'I only saw her for a second but I'm as sure as one ever can be,' she said. I decided not to ask her what she meant. I preferred not to know.

'Can you describe this woman?' the Constable asked.

Momentary glimpse or not, it was immediately evident that she could. 'I'd put her at a little less than my height, perhaps one metre sixty-five,' said Hannah, who was young enough to have been reared in metric. 'She had dark auburn hair with what looked like a natural wave, worn in a ponytail. I was left with the impression of someone who was the thin, nervous type, very intense and possibly intellectual with it. But she wasn't as young as her hair and clothes tried to make out. I would say . . . thirty-five. She wore a grey skirt, rather on the short side, a white blouse and a sort of pinstripe waistcoat.'

'Boring,' Daffy said.

'I thought she looked smart.' (The two girls belonged very much at opposite ends of the fashion spectrum.) 'Oh, and she was carrying one of those stubby, fold-up umbrellas with a black or dark blue cover.'

'That's very good, Miss,' said Buchan. 'Do any of you recognize the description?' He was still writing but I was looking around the faces. Daffy's back was to us — she was putting a plastic container of soup into the microwave oven — but she shook her head without looking round. Henry, Isobel, Hannah, Molly and Sam all looked blank.

'No,' said Noel. I had seen a shift of expression, instantly gone, and for the first time I thought that he might be lying. But I had known him for years. We had shot together and we had a common bond in our affection for Jove. I decided that it was not my business to betray him. Time usually produced the truth. Or buried it. Either would be all right as far as I was concerned.

Constable Buchan returned his attention to me. 'Mobiles have been advised of the theft and of the chance of the dog running loose. The dog was wearing a collar?'

'Of course not,' I said wearily. 'The dog, a particularly biddable Labrador, was in quarantine. It wouldn't have been allowed outside its own run until just now when its owner arrived with the proper authorization to remove it in an approved containment.

We wouldn't expect the car to be stolen. Why would the dog need a collar?'

'I think maybe the question answers itself.' Buchan sighed for the foolishness of mortals. 'Until the car or the dog shows up, there isn't much that we can do.'

Daffy was not usually 'backward in coming forward', but she had been keeping a low profile, probably feeling vulnerable for leaving the car unlocked. Now, however, she piped up. 'Yes, there is,' she said suddenly. 'The woman would have had to get here somehow. Of course, she could have been brought by somebody else. But I've just remembered something. I saw a Lambretta scooter parked outside the gates, pushed half into the hedge. That could be hers. I can't think who else would have brought it. Hang on a moment and I'll get the registration number.'

Buchan's eyes followed Daffy's departing rear view. 'That's a bright girl,' he said wonderingly. Evidently first impressions were being revised — favourably, in the case of Daffy. 'Your car wasn't fitted with Tracker or suchlike?' he asked me.

'You've seen my car,' I said. 'If it was yours, would you spend several hundred quid to make it easier to recover?'

'I see what you mean, sir,' he said — politely enough, but the curl of his lip suggested that he might have paid somebody several hundred quid not to recover it.

Daffy returned, slightly breathless, and quoted the letters and digits to Buchan. 'I left it where it was,' she said. 'There was a crash-hat dangling from the handlebar — adjusted to quite a small size, if that's any help.'

While Buchan phoned the information to his superiors, we began to turn our attention to the mundane trivia of living.

Due to the unpredictability of dogs and clients, we could never be sure who or how many would be present for a meal, so by custom whoever was around and free at the time coped with the need for food. In the process of training dogs for the gun we tended to collect rabbits and pigeon, and gamebirds in season; and vegetables were plentiful around the farms. The freezer was kept stocked with meals prepared by the whole team working as a production line during the occasional slack periods. The large pressure cooker usually held soup in quantity. Hannah, I noticed, was preparing the dogs' meals while Daffy ladled soup into mugs. I was not sure which smelled the better. I was surprised to see that daylight had faded outside.

Noel suddenly snapped his fingers. 'You've put a thought into my head,' he said, 'mentioning Tracker. My mobile phone was in my briefcase. Somebody might have been trying to reach me so I switched the phone on during the taxi ride here. Then I dropped it into my case. But I don't remember switching it off.'

Henry, who had been unusually silent, looked up from his soup. 'The battery was freshly charged? How long does it usually last, switched on?'

'About half a day,' Noel said. 'Perhaps a little more if there aren't many calls. I have a high capacity battery. Cellfone can work out which area you're in, can't they?'

Henry always carries the most extraordinary information in his head. 'As long as your phone's switched on and within range of a station,' he said, 'its signal's registered in the central computer so that the network knows which base station it's nearest to. But it isn't information that they hand out liberally.'

'I do know that they've helped out in kidnap cases,' said the Constable doubtfully.

'This *is* a kidnap case,' I pointed out.

Henry spared me no more than a pitying glance. 'If the police approach them through channels,' he said, 'the battery will be dead before they get around to it. I used to know the managing director. Where's your cordless?' Henry, during his working life, had been a departmental manager in a merchant bank and his range of acquaintances was almost as broad as his knowledge.

'In the sitting room,' I said. I began to get up to fetch it.

Henry beat me to a standing position. He is very fleet for his years. 'I'll go through there,' he said, picking up his soup mug.

'You don't want us for anything else just now?' Daffy asked Buchan.

Buchan hesitated and then shook his head. 'But don't go away,' he said. 'My Inspector's coming and he'll want to speak to you.'

'That'll be a treat . . . for him!' Daffy looked at me. 'We'd better get on with the evening feed.'

My mind was a long way away from the refinements of dog training. 'Just shovel food into them,' I said. 'We'll worry about their education another day.'

Daffy nodded understandingly. She produced Jove's rubber kangaroo from an unsuspected pocket. 'Here. Just in case he turns up.'

The two girls swallowed their soup and went out to feed the dogs. Beth took Sam away. The room went from crowded to merely occupied.

Isobel moved to the stove. 'I'd better do something about food,' she said. 'Luckily ours is still in the fridge at home, so it won't spoil.' She looked enquiringly at the Constable.

'Thank you kindly,' he said, 'but I'm off duty at ten and my tea will be on the table. I'll just wait for HQ to call me back and then I'll leave you.'

Isobel lit the gas in the grill and looked in the fridge. 'Mixed grill for seven,' she said. Except at weekends, when we like to eat in style and make up for all the snacks and sandwiches, we keep things flexible.

'What about your plane?' I asked Noel.

He blinked at me for a moment and then at his watch. 'Oh, bugger my plane!' he said at last. 'Pardon my French! Jove is far more important. If I may, I'll go and use your phone when Mr Kitts has finished.'

Henry came back a minute or two later, sniffed the air appreciatively and said, 'He's trying to get hold of the right technician. He'll call me back.'

'I won't keep the line busy, then,' said Noel. 'What are our chances?' he asked Buchan.

The Constable shrugged. 'We don't get much joy-riding hereabouts,' he said. 'The car isn't exactly the sort to be stolen for its value nor for use as a get-away car. Frankly, it's most likely to have been stolen for its contents.'

'A dog, an attaché case probably full of Mr Cochrane's dirty socks and an old and clapped-out shotgun that nobody knew was there,' I said. 'Not even a radio.'

'You could have been seen from a distance, putting any or all of them into the car,' said Buchan.

'A dog has little cash value without its pedigree,' said Isobel.

'It may have a wheen of sentimental value. Folk have been known to fall for a dog from a distance. And shotguns have their uses,' Buchan said grimly.

'Shotguns are very rarely stolen for use in crime,' I said with some heat. The persecution of legitimate gun-holders as an inexpensive sop to public concern was a subject on which I held strong views. 'There's a huge black market in guns which have never been legally held.'

'Not everybody has access to the black market,' Buchan retorted. 'It may have been stolen for an act of hatred or revenge.'

'Do you mean hatred of or revenge against me personally?' I asked him. 'I seem to be suffering more than anybody outside this household. Or did you mean in order to shoot somebody?'

'I hadn't thought of the first,' Buchan said. 'Have you made any enemies?'

'Who hasn't?'

Buchan took my question for a statement. 'True enough. And tell me, Mr Cochrane, what was in your briefcase?'

'Toothbrush and pyjamas, spongebag, the dirty socks Mr Cunningham mentioned, my mobile phone plus some papers that wouldn't interest anybody outside the firm.'

'And the firm is . . . ?'

'Cook and Simpson Pharmaceuticals,' Noel said. Although it was no secret, I thought that he disgorged the information reluctantly.

Buchan was on the point of asking another question when the telephone sounded its electronic note. The Constable answered it, spoke a few words and then disconnected.

'The scooter was reported stolen in Glasgow yesterday, so there is little help to be gained there. But there is also a report of a car on fire in the lay-by just this side of the village of Myresie,' he said. 'The Inspector has gone straight there. He would like you to go and see if you can identify it.'

'Oh, shit!' Noel said, softly but audibly.

Two

There was a moment of suspended animation while we weighed the ramifications. Noel put our cordless phone down on the table very gently, as if silence was imperative. Beth had come back while the Constable was on the phone. 'Is there any sign of a dog?' she asked urgently.

'Not that they told me,' said Buchan.

'Take my car,' Henry said. He gave me the keys. Constable Buchan, who had been assuming that duty required him to offer transport and envisaging a long night of it, gave a sigh of relief. 'And you'd better have this,' Henry added, handing over his own slimline mobile phone. He had managed a lengthy business career without any such aids, he once said, but at Isobel's insistence had carried a Yuppiphone ever since his first heart attack caught him alone and in the countryside.

It seemed to be assumed that Noel and I would go. Beth got between us and the door and grabbed Henry's car keys off me. 'You are not going off into the night hungry and cold,' she said. 'Either of you.'

It would have been useless to protest that we had only just finished our mugs of soup. When Beth uses that tone even head keepers toe the line and I could see that Noel recognized *force majeure* as well as I did. In what seemed like seconds she had furnished us each with a bacon roll, the bacon hot from the pan already sizzling on the stove, while Isobel filled a Thermos flask with coffee. Beth dropped the keys into my pocket and gave me a nod of dismissal.

I gobbled my sandwich between the house and Henry's car. We belted ourselves in and I drove off into the darkness.

'How far is this place?' Noel asked. He was still working on his sandwich and his voice was muffled.

'Maybe fifteen miles,' I said.

'God! I hope Jove's all right.'

That went without saying. I settled down to burn up the road. The old car had not owed me anything and I was not overly concerned about Noel's briefcase; but Jove was important, as much for his own sake as for the implications of his removal from quarantine. As for the shotgun, I had had Old Faithful since my boyhood but had rarely used it since acquiring a much more up-market gun; perhaps a good blaze would have accomplished deactivation within the meaning of the law and got me off that particular legal hook.

Noel said no more but he was muttering to himself perhaps in prayer. The road was a narrow and twisting country road but I blazed down the tunnel of our lights and covered the fifteen miles in not many more minutes. We came out on a more important road. I knew where to find the lay-by, a loop of old road left stranded behind a string of trees when the road was straightened. Any glow of flames in the sky had died away but there was some reflected lamplight and the blink of a blue lamp which died as we approached. As we came closer the stink of burned rubber and paint and plastic filtered into Henry's car.

There were tapes across the mouth of the lay-by. I could see two cars at least beyond the tapes and a group of men, some in uniform and some not. A uniformed officer halted me and came to the window.

'The lay-by's closed,' he said.

'I was sent for,' I said. 'That might be my car. Has a dog been found?'

He became more human. 'Not that I know.' He lowered his voice. 'But pigs will fly the day they tell me anything.' He lifted the tapes and I parked just beyond as directed.

As soon as I was out of the car I fished out my dog-whistle and blew a rapid series of short blasts, the almost universal 'come' signal. Among the men's voices and the sound of a passing van, the 'silent' whistle was inaudible.

Noel got out and waited beside me, but the dark figure which arrived in apparent answer to my whistle was not an affectionate black Labrador but another uniformed policeman, rather more senior to judge from the silver that glittered on his shoulder. 'Mr Cunningham?' he said.

'I am,' I said. I raised my hand so that he would see which figure the voice was coming from. 'And this is the owner of the dog that was in my car.'

I thought that he nodded in the darkness. 'We've been expecting you both. This way.'

We followed him, but he stopped short of the majority of lights and voices and shone a torch on the remains of an estate car. There was foam on the ground and on the surrounding bushes but the worst had been hosed off the car. It was a sorry sight, a gutted shell.

'Is this your car?' the officer asked. 'Sorry to have to call you out to ask you this, but the number-plates were removed before it was set on fire.'

The feeling that I was attending the funeral of an old friend faded suddenly. 'It's very like it,' I said. 'Same maker. But no. This model came in about three years after mine was built.'

'You're sure?'

'Positive,' I said. 'I looked at my car ten times a day for more years than I care to remember. The roof line's higher and my back window was a slightly different shape.'

I heard the policeman grunt. 'I thought that it was a wee bit too neat,' he said. 'Life's seldom so kind. There seems to be little point to the other part of the exercise but we may as well go through the motions, though you'll not enjoy it. The Fire Brigade was called out to the burning car. When they had it under control, one of the firemen wandered off — for a pee, I think, although he won't admit it because of the implication that he might have had a bladder full of beer. Otherwise what he found might have remained where it is for long enough. A body,' he said at last. 'It's become a long shot, but you'd better look and tell us if you've seen the person before because, if you don't, somebody's bound to ask why not and I'll not have an answer. Come with me.'

We followed his torch again, through a gateway and over grass which felt and smelled damp from the evening dew; and traced a rough semicircle designed to take us by the route least likely to contain any useful tracks. We returned almost to the lay-by. The last few yards of our route were demarked by stakes and tapes. There was the quick blink of an electronic flash and the photographer backed away onto our leader's toes. 'Sorry, sir,' he said. 'That's the lot.'

The officer tutted without otherwise replying. 'Are you ready?' he asked us. 'Not squeamish about dead bodies?'

He meant well, but I said that I had served in the Falklands and elsewhere. I refrained from adding that I had probably seen far more bodies than he had. It might even have been untrue if he was in Traffic.

Noel was equally familiar with death. 'I started life as a biochemist,' he said.

'That's all right, then. Don't touch anything,' the officer told us. 'Just look.'

The body lay on its side. It had been laid or pushed down between the dry stone wall backing the lay-by and a white enamel bath which was acting as a cattle trough. It was the body of a woman. As best I could tell by the light of a portable lamp, she had dark auburn hair; and it was certainly tied back in a pony-tail. My eyes had adjusted to the darkness and under the bright lamp every detail of her face and clothing was clear and sharp. Her face was unmarked and held little expression, yet I was sure that she had not died peacefully.

I had seen death many times during my service days. It had never lost its sadness but it no longer had the power to shock me. If Noel had developed the same resistance

48

during his laboratory years he had lost it since moving into management. 'I'll wait for you back at the car,' he said shakily. 'I'm only here in case my dog turns up.'

The officer agreed absently. His attention was all on me. 'You've seen her before?' he suggested.

'Only in my mind's eye,' I told him. 'But she matches the description of the woman who stole my car. Matches it very closely. I know it doesn't make a whole lot of sense, but if you send for Hannah, my kennel-maid, we can settle the matter straight away. She had a good look at the woman and gave us the description.'

'Very well.' He led me back to the gate-way. On the way, I blew my silent whistle again. In the distance a dog barked but it was shrill compared to Jove's deep note. 'I think we still have a constable at your house. He can bring her here,' the Inspector said.

Constable Buchan, I thought, was going to wish that he had accepted the offer of food. Perhaps I could help. It sometimes pays to earn the gratitude of the local bobby. 'I'd better speak to her,' I said. 'She might panic if she's suddenly whisked away by a strange man even if he is in uniform. Then I can wait and reassure her and take her home again.'

'That sounds sensible.'

I took out Henry's phone and groped for the on-switch. Obligingly, the keypad lit itself up. I was not well acquainted with mobiles — such devices ranked fairly low on our list of future extravagances — but I knew enough to preface my home number with the area code and finish with the 'pick-up' key. Beth answered.

'Put Hannah on, please,' I said.

'All right. Is it — was it — our car?'

'No. Put —'

'So there's no sign of Jove?'

'None at all.' One of my personal quirks, that of being thrifty with phone calls, dated from my childhood. It was redoubled on Henry's mobile. Henry never seemed to concern himself over the cost, but I knew that as a moderate user he had opted to pay a low rental for the connection and a high cost per minute for calls. I had a mental picture, only slightly exaggerated, of golden coins dribbling into a slot. 'I'll tell you all about it when I see you,' I said. 'Let me speak to Hannah.'

'In a moment. Here's Henry.'

'I spoke to my friend at Cellfone,' said Henry's voice. 'The technician he wants seems to have vanished into London's nightlife but he's trying to get hold of him.'

'I see. Put Hannah on.'

Hannah came on the line at last. Quickly, I explained to her that she should let Constable Buchan chauffeur her to me and I pressed the 'hang-up' key before the policeman beside me could ask to speak to Buchan. Without comment, he used his radio to convey the order.

We waited.

The officer, who finally introduced himself as Inspector Tirrell, seemed to accept that I was palpably innocent, a victim rather than a culprit, because he became unusually forthcoming for a policeman. He had a pleasantly deep voice which came out of the darkness without any noticeable accent, but the glimpses that I had of his face, as lights and cars came and went, left me with a confused picture of a man designed by Picasso and executed by Dali.

'You'll have your hands full, with a murder on them,' I suggested. 'You don't have to let me take up your time. I'll bring Hannah to you when she arrives.'

I heard a sound in the darkness which I took to be the proverbial mirthless laugh. 'There's a detective super on the way,' he said. 'Meanwhile, I'm the senior officer present but a detective sergeant's directing the real work. I ken fine how it'll be. I'll be left with stolen or burning cars to deal with and maybe a missing dog.' He gave another snort of something that wasn't quite laughter. 'The car will be cool enough for us to read the engine and chassis numbers, but

I could make a good guess at them now.'

'You could?' I said. 'How?'

I thought that he smiled. 'Word came through, just before you got here, of another of this make stolen near Perth.'

Noel had probably been somewhere nearby in the darkness. He materialized suddenly at my elbow. 'There's nothing to keep me here,' he said, 'but I won't travel too far in the hope that Jove may turn up. I seem to remember that there's a decent pub in Myresie Village.'

'I can recommend it,' said the Inspector.

'I'll walk along there,' Noel said. I offered to drive him and return, but he declined. 'Thanks, but it's not very far —'

'About half a mile,' Inspector Tirrell said helpfully.

'And I don't even have a bag to carry. I'll have to stock up again from the village shop in the morning — unless you've worked a miracle by then, Inspector. I can manage for one night. We'll keep in touch.'

'I'm sorry all your plans have been upset in this way,' I said. I felt vaguely guilty for the loss of his dog and his case. I was relieved that we had not been obliged to offer him a bed. The house was crowded enough at the best of times and guests tended to disrupt the smooth running of the kennels. Noel's presence would have been a constant reminder of the tension

52

engendered by questions of guilt and blame.

'Not your fault,' he said gruffly. 'Good night.' And he trudged away into the darkness.

I turned to the faint outline of the Inspector. 'As your constable was at pains to point out, my car was too old and tired to be wanted for the black market and not fast or reliable enough to be used in a robbery. We don't get many joyriders around here, do we?'

'Not a lot,' he said. 'Not up here at what you might call the respectable end of Fife. Rather more in the southwest. Of course, they could have come over from Dundee.'

I rather doubted that. Even the helpful provision of a bridge across the Firth of Tay had not tempted the bad hats of Dundee to pay us much attention. Fife had always been as remote as the moon to them. 'Why would they set a car on fire?' I asked. 'It seems so wanton.'

He leaned back against the nearest car and folded his arms. 'Criminals do it to make sure they've eradicated all traces of themselves. That much I can understand. Joyriders do it because it rounds off the trip. With them it's just what you said, wanton.'

I am always ready to be interested by the ins and outs of another person's expertise and I would have kept him chatting if I could, but a Range Rover in some nondescript colour came through the tapes and my companion hurried away. I gathered that the Detective Superintendent had arrived to take over. I was left alone with the noises of the night. There was an owl in the distance. Nearer, a rabbit squealed suddenly. I tried the whistle again but this time got no response at all.

A few minutes later a small panda car made a much less impressive arrival. The interior light came on and I saw that Constable Buchan had arrived with Hannah.

I gave Hannah a pull to get up out of the car and she held on to my hand for reassurance. 'I'll fetch her home again,' I told Buchan. 'You get on back before your tea gets cold.'

He hesitated, wondering whether his defection would merit a black mark. Hunger triumphed over ambition. He reversed, turned and drove back the way he had come.

Inspector Tirrell excused himself and broke away from a group huddle. As he joined us, I said to Hannah, 'They're going to ask you to look at a body, in case it's somebody you've ever seen before. Can you manage? It's not a pleasant sight, but not too dreadful either.'

She swallowed. 'Will you come with me?'

'If you like.'

'All right, then. Can we get it over quickly, please?'

Tirrell led us by the same roundabout route. The stakes and tapes marking the pathway had been extended and there were more lamps around the body. Hannah took one look and nodded. I drew her away, Inspector Tirrell following.

'That's her,' Hannah said. 'The woman who drove off in Mr Cunningham's car this afternoon.'

'You're absolutely sure?' Tirrell asked.

'I'm in no doubt that she's the same woman,' Hannah said carefully, 'although I can't swear that she drove the car away. I'd have recognized her face. Even her clothes are the same.'

'But no umbrella,' I said.

We explained the umbrella to Tirrell, who went off to consult some of the lower ranks and came back. 'No umbrella's been found,' he said. 'It'll probably turn up when we have daylight. Come and make a statement.' His voice and manner were avuncular. Hannah could have been ten years old and shy. Before she let go of my hand I felt her relax.

I would have followed on their heels but the phone in my pocket began to make noises. I took it out and found the right key. Henry came on the line. 'Your dinner's in the oven and getting dried up. Your wife wants to know when you're coming for it.'

'Tell her that I said you could have it,' I told him. 'This looks like being a long night.'

'What's going on?'

I compressed the bare facts into the minimum of words.

'But still no dog?' Henry asked.

'No dog,' I confirmed. Everybody seemed to be more concerned about Jove than about me. Come to think of it, I felt the same.

I pressed the 'hang-up' key and settled in Henry's car, broached the coffee and started the engine for the sake of a little extra warmth. The night was turning cold and I had left in too much of a hurry to think of a coat.

Our part in the investigation was finished more quickly than I expected. Hannah sat in the Detective Superintendent's Range Rover and dictated her statement to a sergeant who, she said later, seemed more interested in establishing a flirtatious relationship. The Superintendent, a lean man with a suspicious manner, sent for me to answer a few pointed questions.

After that, we were free to go. It might be a puzzle as to why a woman who had made off with one stolen car should be found near the burned remains of another, but that mystery was clearly the exclusive province of the police and none of our damn business.

Inspector Tirrell, taking his line from his superior, confirmed that he would be in touch as soon as he had news of my car or of Jove. He was less forthcoming than earlier when I tried to pump him about the cause of the woman's death and went so far as to thank us coldly for our cooperation and hint very firmly that we should now go and leave the real people to their real tasks. His reticence was of no real concern to me. My question had arisen out of no more than idle curiosity. I had seen more than my share of those dead by violence. A blow to the back of the head can have a very definite effect on the eyes. Among other incidents, one of my corporals had slipped and fallen down a rock-face, crushing the back of his skull. The signs were the same.

Hannah was unlike her usual communicative self as I drove slowly home. A first sight of death is a terrifying confirmation of one's own mortality and a reminder of uncertainties about the fundamentals of existence. One's own shell may be empty some day. Not 'will', please note, but 'may'. Absolute finality is unacceptable, especially for the young.

I had used Henry's phone to warn of our return, so a fresh meal awaited me in the Three Oaks kitchen along with Beth, Isobel,

Henry and Daffy, each bursting with overt, and to my mind morbid, curiosity. Beyond confirming that she had recognized the dead woman as having been the thief of my car, Hannah seemed unwilling to talk and soon took herself off to bed. Daffy seemed to be torn between following her in order to extract a fuller account of her experiences, going off to bed, or remaining in the kitchen with us. Despite the early start that her job called for every morning, she opted for the kitchen.

If they expected startling facts or speculation from me they were doomed to disappointment. The signs of death from a whack on the back of the skull were not, in my old-fashioned view, for ladies — even for Isobel, who could discuss the detailed symptoms of pyometra in a canine womb without turning a hair. I told them what little I knew and left it at that.

Isobel's hideous spectacles flashed at me. 'The whole thing would make some sort of sense if it had been your car that was found burning,' she said. She glanced sidelong at Daffy. 'The lady hadn't been interfered with?'

To my mind a lethal blow constituted serious interference, but Isobel's mind was running on more feminist lines. 'If she had,' I said, 'she had been tidied up again.'

'Then I'm baffled.'

'I expect so,' Henry said. 'But then, you do baffle rather easily.' Isobel, from the other end of the kitchen table, pretended to throw something at him and he chuckled.

'You can offer us an explanation, I suppose,' Isobel said.

Henry nodded cheerfully. 'I think so, in the light of what we know so far. A theory, at least. Think about it. The modern car's very easily and commonly stolen. It's also very easily traced. So only the most rash or amateurish of criminals setting out to commit a crime uses his own car.'

'Then you think that there's a professional criminal involved?' Beth asked.

'Not necessarily. Lots of people know how to get into a car. Garage mechanics. Policemen. Private detectives. Security men. Plus, of course, anybody who comes across a car left outside the owner's house with the doors unlocked and the engine ticking over.'

'You don't expect —' Daffy began. She had flushed scarlet.

'It's all right,' I said. 'We don't blame you.'

'I certainly don't,' Henry said, beaming paternally. He had always had a soft spot for Daffy. Sometimes I wondered what sort of a young man Henry had been. 'We've all left a car outside our front door with the key in it at some time. So,' he resumed, 'anyone embarking on a foray, during which he or she may have to step outside the law; is likely to equip themselves with a vehicle which has been — shall we say? — borrowed without the owner's agreement. And, because recent advances in forensic science have made it easy to prove that somebody has been in a certain place or a certain car, as often as not they set fire to the car when they've finished with it.

'The lady, whoever she was, may have been after one of several things. She was unlikely to have known that your gun was in the car although anyone keeping watch from the road or the Moss could have seen Daffy secrete the gun under the back seat. In order to transport something that couldn't be carried by scooter, she may have wanted any old car.'

'Mine certainly fits that description,' I said.

'How true! She may have wanted Jove, although that seems unlikely. I suppose it's just conceivable that Mr Cochrane had sold him and then refused to deliver, but in that case she would hardly have chosen to arrive by stolen scooter, if that's what she did. On the whole I think it's almost certain that she was after something that she believed, rightly or wrongly, to be in the attaché case.'

'But that doesn't explain —' Isobel began.

Henry rolled on. 'Having got away with the car and its contents, she drove to the lay-by. She wanted to look for the item she was after. It may be that she had an alternative means of transport waiting there.'

'In which case,' I said, 'where is it? Assuming that her killer drove off in my car —'

'There may have been more than one of him,' Henry said irritably. 'Or her. Try not to interrupt. Where was I?'

'At the lay-by,' Daffy said.

'Oh, yes. She may merely have stopped to check that she had got what she came after. Her killer or killers arrived in another stolen car. Either she had seen too much or else there was a fight over possession of the goodies. She got herself killed, poor girl. According to John, knocked on the head.

'By that time, darkness was falling. Daffy had moved the shotgun to a hiding place under the back seat to make space, had put Mr Cochrane's case into the underfloor compartment — a compartment that not everybody knows about although it's a standard feature in that make of car — and had then dumped a heavy dog in a far from lightweight crate and a travelling box on top of it.

'At first glance he, she or they, couldn't find what they were after, which they may have seen from a distance being carried to the car. Rather than hang about with two stolen cars and a dead body, they preferred to switch to John's car. And then they set fire to the other car in case their fingerprints — traditional or the DNA variety — proved their connection to what had become a murder.'

'That's quite good,' Isobel said. 'You're turning quite logical in your old age. But . . .'

'Yes?'

'Leave it,' Isobel said. 'We're straying into the area of the macabre and I don't want to upset any young stomachs at this time of night.'

'I don't upset very easily,' Daffy said. 'If I can help you sew up a dog that's ripped its bowel on barbed wire, words are hardly likely to make me throw up.'

'I suppose that's true.' The unsuitable spectacles, which made her look like somebody's maiden aunt, flashed in the artificial light. 'Well, my question is, if they were going to burn the car why didn't they burn the body with it?'

Henry stretched and yawned. 'Now you're inviting me to make wild guesses as to what was in a murderer's mind just after the deed. One guess might be that she seemed to have given up John's car peacefully. She may even have met them by arrangement or arrived at a subsequent agreement.

Then, after they had fired the other car and as they were about to drive away in yours, she made some extra demand. Perhaps she threatened them with John's shotgun. It wouldn't have been loaded, unless she happened to have a few cartridges in her handbag, but they mightn't know that. After they'd killed her, it would be much more difficult to put her body into a car that was already on fire and would at any moment attract the attention of the emergency services. And now, it's after our bedtime and I think we should walk home. We'll leave our car with you, John, in case there are any more emergencies.'

'Which God forbid,' I said. I thought that somebody murmured a heartfelt, 'Amen!'

Three

My illness a few years earlier had destroyed the sleep pattern which had been a vital part of my army life. I was slowly recovering the blessing of deep sleep, but after a day that seemed, in retrospect, to have been taken up by crime and the police, and with the legal implications of Jove and my gun to fret me, I slept fitfully that night, only falling deeply asleep at last as the dawn chorus began outside the window.

In deference to my still uncertain health I was sometimes allowed to sleep late. By the time I came downstairs, the work of the kennels was well under way. While I saw to my own breakfast Isobel, hurrying indoors to collect some veterinary product, explained that one of our brood bitches had brought back fleas from stud and passed them on to several of her colleagues. I had been favoured with a late morning because it had been decided by the ladies of the business — that is to say, everybody but myself — that there would be no training that day. Instead every dog, bitch and pup would be bathed, blow-dried, de-ticked and treated with a separate insecticide. (Due to yet another miracle of bureaucratic incompetence, there was not a single insecticidal shampoo with EC approval for sale in Britain that year.)

Henry had walked over with Isobel and he joined me for a second if smaller breakfast. 'The technician at Cellfone rang me just before we left home,' he said.

'And?'

I had to wait until he had swallowed a mouthful of toast and marmalade. 'That technician seems to be a real whiz,' he said. 'He could backtrack the movements of a phone and tell you the colour of the user's socks, but unfortunately there's no way to tell exactly where the phone is, only which cell it's in.

'Cochrane's phone remained in this area until the small hours of this morning. Then it was switched off.'

'A pity,' I said.

'Yes. Presumably it had been found — whether by the killer, the current possessor of your car or some third party, we have no way of knowing.'

'Or even by some passing tramp who found it where one of the others had discarded it.'

'Unlikely at that stage,' Henry said kindly. 'Later, it was switched on again and a call was attempted, but the connection was never made and they have no record of the intended recipient. All he could tell me was that the phone remained switched on for some minutes, perhaps in the hope of a call that never came, and he was able to determine that the phone was still in this cell but was also detectable through another. He suggests that we look for it somewhere along the south bank of the Tay, roughly between Perth and the sea.'

It was my turn to empty my mouth before speaking. 'That's a hell of a lot of bank,' I said. 'And presumably he doesn't mean just the foreshore.'

'God, no!' Henry said. 'They're cagey about the exact areas covered by their cells but I gathered that he narrowed it down by determining that the signal couldn't be detected by the next base station to the south. He suggested a margin of twenty miles.'

'Useless!'

'Better than nothing. At least we know that it's still in the area,' Henry pointed out.

I could have replied that the phone might by now be on some rubbish dump, with my car and Jove five hundred miles away, but I decided that the mood was gloomy enough. Henry just managed to beat me to the last slice of toast. I got up to make some more. So it was going to be that sort of day!

'I have more news,' Henry said. 'After my

call from the technician was finished, my friend the boss-man of Cellfone called, sounding harassed. The police had been on to him for much the same information and of course he had had to give it to them. But then there was another request. He wouldn't say who from, but he did let out that it was from a very big client. Having helped us, he could hardly not help somebody he depends on for a great deal of business; conversely, he agreed that if he wouldn't tell us the identity of the other enquirer he wouldn't tell them of our interest.'

'And the police?' I asked.

'The police had already been given what they wanted before the other enquiry came in. He doesn't want to make any enemies.'

I wanted to go back to bed. Life was becoming altogether too complicated. We sat and drank coffee in moody silence.

The cordless phone was beside me. When it rang, I flinched. I was expecting calls from the half-dozen different officials who could be counted on to come at me for losing a shotgun or an animal out of quarantine. But the call was from Constable Buchan, who was beginning to seem quite friendly in comparison with all the bureaucrats who would want to jump up and down on my body before very long.

'I may have news of your car,' he began.

I nearly told him to stuff my car. The car had faded into minor importance. 'What about Jove and my shotgun?' I asked.

'That I wouldn't know. The car's still mostly under water. You know the slipway at Lindhaven?'

I said that I did.

'There's a car in the mud at the bottom of the slip, only partly showing at low tide. The colour's right, that's all I can say. They're trying to get frogmen out to get a cable on it. You may care to go along.'

I thanked him and broke the connection. 'I heard that,' Henry said. 'Shall I go?'

The thought of staying at home to cope with irate officialdom or else becoming involved in a mass dog-bath, with some dogs howling because they hated being bathed and others trying to go through the process again, and all of them determined to shake themselves over me, was too debilitating to contemplate.

'We'll both go,' I said.

He looked at me reproachfully with his ancient, bloodhound's eyes. 'You ought to stay. The council will be coming after you about Jove.'

'That's why I'm coming with you. Beth's a partner. She can cope.'

'And the Divisional Veterinary Officer?'

'Isobel can deal with him. She'll probably make him help bath the dogs. I think he fancies her. And after all, she's his deputy.' This was true. Isobel had been appointed as a deputy divisional veterinary officer, to carry out the required routine visits to the previous local quarantine kennels and when their licence had transferred to us nobody had thought to change the arrangement.

Henry was not through yet. Although not a partner in the firm he was always ready to help and he had coped with much of the paperwork when we applied for the licence. He knew the Standard Requirements and the Conditions to be Observed better than I did. 'And the police?' he said.

I heaved a deep sigh. 'On two counts,' I said, 'I would rather be a long, long way away. Regarding Jove, Beth and Isobel can cope. And if the Firearms Officer comes round about my gun, I'd rather not be here. With a bit of luck, I may get it back along with the car before he catches up with me, which will put me on a much stronger footing.'

I telephoned the pub at Myresie and asked for Noel Cochrane. He had stayed the night but had left after an early breakfast. They were not expecting him back. And no, he had not left any forwarding address.

Tacitly, we agreed that our wives would prefer not to be interrupted in mid-dog-bath. I wrote a note explaining where we had gone and why. We left it on the kitchen table and went out into the sunshine.

I drove Henry's car. Henry may deny that he is now in his old age, except when he wants to spend the money which he and Isobel had been saving for it or to make some other point, but he does admit that his confidence in his own driving ability is less than it was. No man enjoys being driven in his own car but Henry was usually relaxed when I drove him. That day he had the fidgets but not, I discovered, because of my driving.

'It could be worse,' he said at last.

I was not in a mood for looking on the bright side. The more I thought about it the greater the number of imminent disasters I could see looming. 'Could it? Tell me how.'

'Jove could develop rabies.'

He was right. It could be worse.

We took to the narrow roads closest to the big estuary. Soon we could see the broad expanse of water sparkling under the sun, beyond it the Carse and in the far distance the Sidlaw Hills. The village of Lindhaven is no more than a tiny cluster of houses with a shop which also serves a scattering of farms and holiday cottages. The slipway is a natural slot cut down through the bank, which at that point is twenty feet above the river bed, by a stream which was later culverted and the resulting surface paved with stones.

A large recovery vehicle was blocking the road half a mile short of the village, straddling the bridge where the stream plunged underground. Beyond, I could see a police Range Rover painted in the usual jam-sandwich livery. A policeman came to my window. 'You'll have to wait, sir,' he said. He had to speak up over the din of the recovery vehicle's engine. I saw that a cable leading down the slipway was being reeled in under the eyes of a few interested spectators. 'We're pulling a car out of the Tay.'

'I know,' I said. 'It may very well be my car.'

His expression became almost sympathetic. Nobody had bothered to tell him that I was now an outcast. 'Mr Cunningham? Inspector Tirrell's expecting you.' He showed me where I could park.

Tirrell arrived as we got out of Henry's car. Now that I saw him in daylight, he was nearing middle age and lightly built for a policeman. He was in uniform and capped, but the hair at his neck and sideburns was sandy and matched a fine crop of freckles. His bony face bore an expression suggesting great patience, but I thought that there might be a temper somewhere, deeply buried. He greeted us politely which, I thought, was more than I could expect from his colleagues responsible for firearms or for policing the Animal Health Act 1981.

'You may find your shotgun more or less intact,' he said. 'I wouldn't count on anything else. The car's a definite write-off.'

A writing-off following a well-attested theft should satisfy even the most pettifogging insurance company. The prospect of some insurance money to help replace a car which had been long overdue for replacement brought a tiny gleam of sunshine back into my day, but I felt obliged to protest for the look of the thing. 'Surely,' I said, 'a dunking in salt water . . .'

'Whoever suggested that that was the extent of the damage was seriously misinformed,' Tirrell said. 'We're hauling it out by way of the slipway but that isn't how it went in. Come this way.' He led us to the bank above the slip. Faint tyre tracks led from the road across rough grass to where the edge showed raw earth. Something reminiscent of my old car, my faithful steed of many years, was crawling painfully crabwise up the slipway, spewing mud and groaning pathetically. 'He drove it to the very brink,' Tirrell said, 'got out and let the slight slope do the rest. Nobody heard anything, but a fisherman, launching an inflatable at first light, spotted the wheels sticking up. The car was on its roof but we've managed to right it.'

Henry was looking around. 'Too dry for

footprints?' he asked.

'I'm afraid so. And I don't hold much hope of a lot of forensic evidence even if the car does turn out to be connected to the murder.'

A large dollop of mud fell off the front of the car. 'No number-plates once again,' I remarked.

'Removed,' said Tirrell, 'either in the hope of delaying identification, which seems unlikely, or to stick on the next car stolen in order to confuse us. Can you identify your own car?'

'Probably,' I said. 'Let's have a closer look.'

We descended to the head of the slip and picked a way carefully down it. Inspector Tirrell left us to have a word with the driver of the recovery vehicle.

The remains came to a halt and were left while the vehicle was manoeuvred into a new position. I studied the car from close to. Some glass had gone, and Tay mud, which I knew from my wildfowling experience to be the smelliest and most glutinous mud to be found around the coast of Britain, had coated much of the inside and filled the footwells. What I could see through the mud coating looked like a perversion of my car but the back was empty. I dragged open a door and fumbled cautiously inside. The locker under the floor at the back held only muddy water. I tackled the rear seat, heaving the back up towards its usual position. Some rusty remains sulked underneath.

I straightened, holding out my hands so as not to transfer more mud than necessary to my person. 'I identify the car,' I said, 'and that's my shotgun under the seat.'

'I'll have to take the gun in charge for the moment,' Tirrell said. 'You'll probably get it back eventually.'

'I shan't hold my breath,' I said sadly. 'It's an old friend but it was never a "Best" gun and after a night in salt water I don't suppose it'll ever fire again. I'd be glad to have it back and deactivated as a wall-hanger. There's a host of good memories attached to it. I assume that nothing's been removed? The men that found the car didn't rescue a dog? Or find a dead one?'

'It was as you saw it.'

'With the back closed?'

'Just as you saw it,' Tirrell repeated.

The driver of the recovery vehicle lent me a rag with which to wipe off the worst of the mud. 'What about the boxes?' I asked. 'For transporting quarantined dogs we operate what they call "System A". Instead of a special vehicle we have a box within a crate. The outer crate is big. It fills most of the back of the car, which is why the bag was stowed under the floor and the gun moved to where it is.'

'Ah,' said Inspector Tirrell. 'And if some-body wanted to search under the floor at the back of the car — for the bag or for something else — how would he go about it?'

'If he cared to lever off two padlocks,' I said, 'he could open the outer crate, lift out the inner container complete with dog and then heave out the empty crate. But the inner travelling box is a damned awkward lift from the outer one with a dog inside, unless the dog and the box are small. Both the fronts let down. When loading up, we usually prefer to put them both in the car, one inside the other, before introducing the dog. And then we reverse the procedure when getting them out again.'

'In that case,' Tirrell said slowly, 'I want to show you something. It's a good step back along the road and I prefer to leave my driver on guard here. Will you give me a lift?'

'Of course,' I said. His mention of his driver being on guard made me wonder whether somebody who had failed to find what they wanted in my car might not be lurking in wait for another chance. I lowered my voice. 'I suppose those rubber-necks are all genuine locals?'

As soon as the words were out I felt sure that I had made a fool of myself but the Inspector took me seriously. 'I checked,' he said.

Henry was relegated to the back seat of his own car and Tirrell joined me in the front. I drove back the way we had come. 'Not far now,' Tirrell said. 'I noticed something when we passed by on the way here. It didn't seem meaningful at the time.'

'I think that I'd have seen and recognized our crate,' I said.

'Remember that I had the advantage of being driven. And I was higher up in the Range Rover. That extra foot or two of height makes all the difference when it comes to seeing over hedges and dykes. Stop here.'

I pulled onto the verge. Beside the road an expanse of rough ground, fringed with grass but mostly beaten down to bare earth and gravel and backed by trees, was partly screened by overgrown gorse bushes. A rusty three-gang plough and some straw bales suggested that a farmer used this otherwise wasted corner for overflow storage, as was a common local practice. Very rarely did any equipment disappear.

We got out of the car. The sweet smells of spring were all around. I used my whistle, but to no effect.

When we rounded the biggest clump of gorse I saw that our large crate and a travelling box stood open on the grass. Nearby, completely hidden from the road, was the body of a man.

Inspector Tirrell went down on his knees beside the body, which was lying on its side in the grass. To my relief, I saw that the man was breathing. There were ants on his face, his skin looked grey and only a sliver of white showed at each eye; but he was only in his twenties and, in better circumstances, must have been good-looking. His clothes would not have looked out of place on one of the better golf courses except that they had suffered from contact with the ground.

It seemed unfair to watch him as he lay with his mouth open, dribbling slightly, so I looked around me. The crate and the box, I noticed, were open and empty and there was no sign of a dog. The hasps, twisted and broken and with the padlocks still in place, lay nearby. I could see faint tyre tracks in the dirt and also irregular marks which might have been left by a struggle, or by almost anything else.

'He's cold but he's alive,' Tirrell said. 'We need an ambulance. Och, dash it! My radio's in the Range Rover. Would you drive back — ?'

'We have a phone,' I told him and he nodded. I borrowed Henry's mobile, keyed nine-nine-nine and asked for an ambulance.

Henry brought a rug from the car and

spread it over the man. Tirrell straightened up thankfully. 'His airway's clear. There's not much more we can do for him until the ambulance arrives. He's in a bad way. Knocked on the head, poor fellow.'

'Like the girl,' I said.

'That's so.' He nodded and then looked at me sharply. 'How did you know the way she was killed?'

'I was in the army,' I said. 'I've seen enough dead and injured.'

As I uttered it, I felt that my answer was lame and unconvincing, but Tirrell seemed to find it more satisfactory than, in his shoes, I would have done. 'I'd forgotten. Falklands, wasn't it?' Tirrell lost interest in me. 'May I have the use of your phone?'

I raised my eyebrows at Henry who nodded but said, 'Go through emergency services again. Ordinary calls cost the earth.'

'The emergency service facilities,' Tirrell said haughtily, 'are not meant for routine traffic.'

'Then you can pay for your calls,' Henry said.

I guessed that it was the paperwork entailed rather than the cost of the calls which made Tirrell's mind up for him. He keyed nine-nine-nine.

Henry's caution was justified. Fifteen minutes trickled by before Tirrell finished passing on information and instructions.

By that time I had my next moves clear in my mind. Without giving Henry time to object, I recovered the phone and keyed the Three Oaks number. I found myself speaking to Beth, who had taken the cordless phone out with her to what she called the salon — the converted outbuilding that housed a warm water spray and a powerful fan-heater.

'Thank God you phoned!' Beth said. 'We're driven mad here. Reporters have been sniffing around. And there was a policeman here about your gun.'

'There would be,' I said. Tirrell had gone down on his knees again in search of an identity for the injured man. I watched over his shoulder. 'Give him a call —'

'I didn't get his name,' Beth said unhappily. 'He did say it, but I was too harassed to take it in.'

'If he calls again then tell him that my shotgun, the one that was in my car when it was stolen, has turned up and is in the care of Inspector Tirrell.'

'Thank the Lord for small mercies! And it is only a small one. So it's our car?'

'It was. It's a write-off. You'd better phone our insurers.'

'No sign of Jove?'

'Not a trace. Just empty boxes about a mile from the car.'

'At least he didn't drown in the car. Shut

up, you daft beggar,' she added. (I thought that the remark was aimed at Bud — short for Buddleia — who I could hear and recognize demanding attention in the background.) 'We've been constantly interrupted by other cops, plus two different men from the District Council and the Veterinary Superintendent.'

'What action are they taking against us?' I held my breath.

'Nothing for the moment.' (I breathed again.) 'Mostly, I think they're waiting to see whether Jove turns up with or without.' She meant with or without rabies.

'The police will be looking for him,' I said, 'but I think it's time we took a hand. The crates turned up near the car, at Lindhaven, so that may be where he was let loose. Leave the rest of the baths to the girls and do some phoning. Speak to the secretaries of the wildfowlers' club and the dog clubs and ask them to notify all their members urgently to keep an eye open for a collarless black Lab on the loose. We'll pay any phone costs or postages. Phone the vets and ask them to pass the word to any clients likely to be dog-walkers. Also all keepers, ghillies, farmers and anyone else you can think of. Nobody's to take any risks, although you can say that he's a very friendly and docile chap. They're to let us know at once and, if possible, lure him with food to somewhere he can be shut in until we get there. All right?'

'I suppose so,' Beth said doubtfully. 'Over what area?'

'Perth to the Road Bridge, from the Tay for twenty miles south.'

'Holy cheeses!'

'Work outwards from Lindhaven,' I said, 'and do the best you can. Ask each person to tell ten others. And offer a reward.'

'How much?'

'I don't know,' I said wearily. Inspector Tirrell was looking in the unconscious man's pockets for identification and had opened his wallet. Over the Inspector's shoulder I was trying to read the name on a firm's identity card which carried a photograph of the man's face. 'Pluck a figure out of the air and double it. Anything would be cheaper than the damage this could cause to our business.'

There was silence at the other end except for the din made by several excited spaniels. 'Is it that bad?' she asked at last. 'Surely they can't blame us for the car being stolen? And if we lost the quarantine authorization, we'd still have all the breeding and training and the boarders.'

'We invested a lot of borrowed money in building work to meet the quarantine standards,' I reminded her. 'If we lose a dog from quarantine and he stays lost, or there's an outbreak of rabies, they'll take another good look at us and maybe notice a few corners that were cut. The approval of our late car as a carrying vehicle, for instance. That was supposed to be temporary.'

'All right,' Beth said. 'I'll do my best.'

I terminated the call with an easier mind. Beth's best is very good indeed. It occurred to me that I had forgotten to mention the unconscious man, but no matter. He was outside the scope of our problems.

Inspector Tirrell, meantime, had thought up some new questions. 'Mr Cochrane's attaché case was put under the floor to make room for the large crate. What happened then?'

I led the Inspector through the procedure for loading an animal out of quarantine, which would have been followed by the two kennel-maids. 'One of them went back to her work,' I finished, 'while the other brought the car to the door, ready for me to drive away.'

'And omitted to lock it,' said Tirrell.

'She expected us to come out immediately,' I said. 'And it might not have made any difference. The modern car thief can get inside any car within fifteen seconds.'

Tirrell looked at me sadly. 'You may get away with that argument or you may not,' he said. 'Luckily for you, that isn't my concern. One man on his own couldn't lift the two crates out of the car complete with dog?'

'Not a hope,' I said. 'It takes two strong men. And you can't even lift out that size of carrying box with a heavy dog inside because it's such an awkward lift and the sides of the crate get in the way of your elbows.'

'So whoever brought your car here would have had to lever open both containers and release the dog before he could empty the back of the car and start the search which seems to have ended with the theft of Mr Cochrane's case?'

'That's it in a nutshell,' I said. 'Perhaps he used the phone from the case to summon somebody to collect him. A confederate, or even a taxi.'

'Perhaps.' Tirrell snapped his mouth shut on the word rather than bandy theories with one who was not in very good odour with the police, but I thought that I saw him make a mental note to follow up the suggestion. There was no time to pump him. An ambulance turned up, closely followed by another Range Rover, this one carrying the Detective Superintendent from the previous night and several subordinates. The lengthy process of waiting around to be asked questions which had already been asked and answered began all over again.

I whistled for Jove several times. I still had his kangaroo in my pocket. At least if he turned up we might be able to fill the time with a few simple retrieving exercises. But the only response was from an old and grubby terrier which came out of the trees, hopeful of being taken for walkies.

Four

The Superintendent, a hatchet-faced man by the name of Easton, finished with us eventually. If he thought it suspicious that I should arrive so early on the scene of both attacks he seemed to accept my contention that I had had a good reason for being there as I had each time been invited to the scene by the police — and that I could account for every moment of my time for several days past.

He seemed less incisive than he had the previous evening. I guessed that he was uncertain whether to demand full control of this secondary case. If the unconscious man either died or recovered and solved the murder for him, then the case was his. In any other event, a mere assault was the province of the humbler Tirrell.

I managed a quick word with Tirrell before Henry and I slipped away. He had been waiting, with more patience than I would have shown, for his superior to go away and get on with his murder case, leaving Tirrell to tidy up such minor matters as the theft of my car and the assault on the man —

whose name, from the card, was Donald something. (Tirrell's thumb had hidden the surname from my inquisitive eyes.)

'Has another car been stolen around here?' I asked him.

Tirrell nodded, in understanding rather than as an affirmative. 'Not so far as I know. I wondered the same thing. Whoever was responsible could have walked far enough before taking another car; but we've had no report from anywhere in Fife. It may not have been missed yet or he may have been picked up. Perhaps he even lives near here. Time may tell but it does seem probable that we're looking for more than one person. The ground's too hard and there have been too many comings and goings for us to read the traces.'

My question had only been a step towards what I really wanted to know. 'What steps are being taken about the missing dog?'

'All officers have been warned not to approach stray dogs but to report them immediately. The SSPCA and certain trained officers will take it from there.'

I felt an uneasiness in my bowels. This sounded very close to my worst fears 'The trained officers being marksmen?' I asked.

He avoided my eye. 'I wouldn't know about that,' he said.

'Surely to God you could at least fix it so that I'll be advised immediately?' I asked. 'I want at least a chance of recovering the animal undamaged. He's valuable and, after all, quarantine is only precautionary. There's no indication whatever that he has rabies and every indication that he doesn't. His owner works for a firm that makes rabies vaccinations, for God's sake! He'd be the last person to take his own dog to the East without immunizing him.'

'I could try to see that you're notified but I couldn't promise,' he said. There was a pause before he added, 'I'm sympathetic. I have a dog of my own.'

He sounded sincere but that was not enough. 'I'm getting the word put around all the dog-walkers and countrymen,' I told him. 'My chances of getting news may be at least as good as yours. But I'm not going to pass the word along so that some trigger-happy cop can be given his first chance at a live target.'

Tirrell's face darkened. 'You have a duty —'

'Bugger my duty!' I said briskly. 'I've spent half my life answering the call of duty and what's it got me? Permanent disability, occasional blackouts and a miserly pension. Now I'm dealing in realistic practicalities, not in what some bobby decides was meant by what some civil servant, who wouldn't know a dog if it bit him, drafted in Whitehall or the Scottish Office. Get me an assurance that I can take charge of any hot search and I'll guarantee — almost guarantee — to locate the dog and to recover him unharmed. By tranquillizer dart if necessary, but I don't think it'll come to that. He knows me well and I trained him. He'll come to my call.'

Tirrell's mouth screwed up in a silent whistle. 'I said that I'd try and I'll do that,' he said. 'If I hear first, I'll let you know. But let me remind you that if you learn of the dog's whereabouts and don't tell us immediately, the consequences could be serious for you.'

'Whatever happens,' I said, 'the consequences could be serious for me. When can I have my crate back, and the travelling box? I don't want them to be abandoned here.'

'Again,' Tirrell said, 'I'll let you know. Tell your insurers that your car can be seen in the police pound at Cupar.'

He turned away. I got into the car with Henry, drove off and stopped at the main road. 'Where the hell has Noel Cochrane got to?' I asked Henry.

'God alone knows,' Henry said gloomily. 'He could be floating face down in the Tay for all we can tell. What may or may not be significant is that the police haven't asked where the hell he's got to.'

A van came up behind me and hooted. I

moved out and drove slowly towards home. 'So what do you deduce? That they have his body? That they have him in custody? That they haven't noticed he's gone? Or that they know where he is and either don't care or don't want us to find out?'

'Any of those,' Henry said, 'and one or two more. Let's stick with things we know for sure.'

'Is there anything we know for sure?'

'Your car will never run again, that's for sure. So you may as well look for a replacement and let me have mine back. What's more, I see that Hugh Morris Motors is advertising interest-free credit at the moment. Business must be slow.'

I found that Henry's car had speeded up without any conscious intent on my part. 'Are they indeed?' I said more cheerfully. What had been an annoyingly bright light had now turned into mildly soothing sunshine. 'And Hugh himself was very interested in one of the dogs, we just couldn't agree the price. Now might be the time for some hard bargaining.'

'Go get him, boy,' said Henry. He folded his arms and leaned back, satisfied.

It was late afternoon before we got back to Three Oaks. We were immediately set upon for absenting ourselves without adequate reason — and not only by our wives.

The kennel-maids, usually half-way respectful to me and in awe of Henry, joined the throng on the gravel outside the front door and let their resentment show with a display of dumb support for the senior ladies. Even Sam, present but reined, seemed to be regarding us with disfavour.

All this disapproval, I could safely assume, was simply anger at our sudden absence. An interruption to my training programme was regarded as my affair and the bathing of the dogs had been completed some time previously; but the dogs' meal-times required all hands or prior warning. Apart from the complexity arising from certain dogs requiring special diets, there were several ancillary tasks. The firing of blank cartridges, for instance, so that young dogs would come to associate the sound of shots with good times and not become gun-shy. Similarly, any pup showing signs of travel sickness was usually fed at the back of one car or another. This was one reason why any car of ours quickly degenerated into a mobile slum. The back of Henry's car was going the same way.

When Beth and Isobel were running out of words I said, 'Finding another body doesn't count as a reasonable excuse?'

'Dead?' Isobel asked.

'Damn near it,' said Henry. 'He'd been hit over the head like the girl and they think he'd been lying there since before dawn. But he was still breathing, after a fashion.'

'Presumably whoever hit him also killed the girl and dumped the car,' Isobel said.

'A facile assumption but probably true. There's no guarantee that he'll come round at all, let alone with any clear memory of who and what and why,' Henry pointed out.

'And you don't know who he is?' said Beth.

'As it happens,' I told her, 'I do know who he is.' (Henry gave me a barbed glance. There had been more interesting topics for discussion in the car.) 'I'll tell you all about it at lowsing time. And about our new car. Also about trading Beech for a substantial part of the purchase price. Beech had better be readied for delivery tomorrow and I'll want the usual pedigree, vaccination certificate and bill of sale.'

They protested but I was adamant, so we went about our business. Beth had been taking advantage of the fine weather and catching up with the gardening chores while keeping an eye on Sam, who was confined behind a mesh fence to a part of the lawn to which dogs were never admitted. The risk of *toxocara canis* was a remote one but, with so many potential carriers around, we were taking no chances. Beth, I noticed, was also on guard against Dover, a randy local mongrel who always had designs on any of our bitches who happened to be within a month either way of her season. For this purpose, Beth kept at her side a boy's catapult and a flowerpot full of round stones. Dover was learning the hard way not to come within fifty yards of her. Beth had a very straight eye.

While I tried to catch up with my schedule for training the younger dogs, the outstanding work was disposed of with unusual energy. Lowsing time, in Scots, is the time for knocking-off from work. We used the term to designate no particular time on the clock but the moment when all tasks were finished and we could gather in the sitting room for a drink and to discuss the events of the day, our plans for the future and, sometimes, the latest gossip of the neighbourhood.

Sam had already been transferred to his playpen. He was beginning to outgrow it and I was thinking in terms of high-level latches on all the doors. Henry acted as barman, as he usually did when he joined our conclave. He helped himself to his customary beer. Isobel took a gin and tonic, Beth a small sherry and Henry poured me the Guinness which was supposed to build me up after my illness. Daffy and Hannah were palmed off with shandy, on the grounds that I had no intention of lavishing the hard stuff on female employees, and young ones at that, except on very special occasions.

'We've phoned everybody in the world,' Beth said rapidly. 'God knows what our next phone bill will look like. But I offered a hundred quid for information leading to the recovery et cetera, so we may be lucky. Now tell us all about it, complete with gruesome details.'

I left it to Henry to tell most of the tale although I had to fill in the details of my talk with Inspector Tirrell. When we had finished there was a thoughtful silence. Even Sam, who would usually fill any conversational gap with his own parody of the English language, seemed to be cogitating.

Beth left the room to check on our dinner, which had been looking after itself on the stove. When she came back, she said, 'You two will have to be careful. There may be somebody going around knocking on the head anyone who gets in his way. The first question to spring to my mind is, did he mean to kill both of them and didn't allow enough for the man's thick skull, or did he just aim for two knockouts and kill the girl by a misjudgment?'

'There's no way of knowing,' I said. 'And don't be sexist. You should say "he or she".'

'Or "they",' said Henry. 'For all we know it was two different people, separately or working in cahoots. The man we found

93

today may even have killed the girl.'

'Mr Cochrane was with us when the girl was killed. I just hope that he didn't have anything to do with the rest of it,' Hannah said.

'Why?'

'Because I rather like him and I don't want to be wrong.'

'The portents aren't very good,' Henry said, 'or where has he gone?'

'He may be lying around somewhere else in the Fife countryside with a lump on his head,' I pointed out.

Beth gave a shiver. 'I'm not even going to think about the possibility. Now tell me, what was that you said about a car? Do we really have a respectable car after all this time?'

'It's not brand new but it's immaculate,' I said. 'Henry will bear me out.'

'Indeed I do,' Henry said. 'Whether a car that carries dogs and gets driven by at least four different people and does a lot of its mileage on estate roads and farm tracks and has dogs sleeping and feeding in the back of it can possibly stay that way is something else again, but you can always hope and pray.'

'At least let's not get it stolen again,' Beth said.

'It shouldn't get stolen,' I said. 'It doesn't have the usual alarms and things that any thief knows how to beat — remember that you can drive around with a burglar alarm honking away these days and nobody pays a blind bit of attention — but the car belonged to some ingenious character who didn't mean to lose it. He fitted a valve in the fuel line, operated by a contactor fed from an otherwise unused switch on the dashboard. So every time you start up you must press that switch once or the car will conk out a few hundred yards up the road. I'll show you, but after that you'll all have to remember. Beth, you'd better call the Agriculture and Fisheries Department in the morning and clear the change of vehicles with them. And two of us can take Beech along tomorrow and bring the car back. No money called for just yet. The cash adjustment's on interest-free credit.'

That set Beth off again, worrying about going back into debt, until Henry reassured her that, guided by his advice, I had for once pulled off a business-like stroke.

We had enough material for the discussion to have lasted for ever, but Sam made it plain that it was high time that he was fed. He was no sooner in full voice than Henry and Isobel set off for home and Hannah and Daffy both remembered urgent tasks which they wanted to complete before dinner. Sam, I thought, was already pulling his weight. He had a powerful pair of lungs.

At some seasons the work of the kennels might go on until long after dark, but we were now at the quietest time of the year, when serious competition was finished, the spring litters were still bulging in their dams' bellies and we were free to do our own things after the evening meal. So when Sam had been given his final toddle in the garden and was bathed and bedded at last, Beth and I settled down in front of the television set in the sitting room.

Irregular hours meant that we usually missed the few good programmes to come on the television. When the business got into the black, one of our first extravagances had been a video recorder. The taped programme that we had chosen that evening could not have been to her liking, but Hannah was sitting with us. Daffy, we gathered, was monopolizing the communal television in the Portakabin.

I found it strange that the two girls failed to get on. It was not that they were different but that they were determined to exaggerate their differences, Hannah intellectual and fastidious, Daffy a punk rebel. Each came from a conventional middle-class home and each had come to work for us directly or indirectly because of a rebellion against the mores of their childhood. They should have been allies against the established world. Instead, although they could work together satisfactorily, they avoided each other in their leisure time. Happily, outbursts were rare but sniping was commonplace.

I would have preferred the science-fiction film which was waiting on tape and would at least have stretched the imagination if adding nothing to worldly culture; but it was Beth's turn to choose and she was rapt in a tearjerker. I was reading and Hannah was beginning to fidget when we heard a car in the drive.

'Who on earth . . . ?' I began.

'It's nobody who ever comes here,' Hannah said. She had the knack of recognizing the sound of many different cars.

The door bell chimed. I stopped the tape, killing the sight and sound of a programme which I would have judged to be aimed at the mentally retarded. But there was nothing wrong with Beth's intelligence. I could only put down the divergence of taste to a difference in hormones.

Hannah hopped up quickly. 'I'll go,' she said. She was soon back, gently closing the door behind her. 'There's a lady,' she said. 'Wants to see you.'

She was looking at me.

'A client?'

Hannah shook her head. 'She wouldn't say what about, but she's not a doggy sort of person, not by a mile.'

'What sort of person, then?'

Hannah's detailed observation of the car thief had not been a fluke. 'A business person,' she said. 'Business dress, anyway. Early thirties, I think. The Amazon type. No rings. Sometimes wears glasses. Blonde hair, dressed very severely. But her car looks quite sporty so I think she must have come straight from work. Her nail varnish is opalescent scarlet. She can probably tart herself up to the nines in minutes when she gets away from the office.'

I felt myself blanch. 'She's not from Ag and Fish, is she?'

Hannah shook her head. 'Some other ministry, perhaps, but not that. Too urban altogether. I doubt if she'd know a welly boot if it trod on her.'

'Or the fuzz?'

'Doesn't have the strut. Business-like but without the arrogance.'

I considered. I was tired and in no mood to be imposed on. But officialdom can have some atypical representatives and client money can take surprising forms. 'I'd better see her,' I said. 'I can take her into the office if you two want to watch telly.'

'I'm going out for a walk,' Hannah said.

'And I can watch the end of the film any time,' said Beth. 'Some time that you're not at home to hate it. If I bother. It's very predictable. I could script the rest of it myself and not be more than a few dozen words adrift. Bring her in here, please, Hannah. And be careful while you're walking,' she added in the direction of Hannah's departing back. 'Take Jason with you. He won't let anyone bother you.' Jason was Beth's personal Labrador. 'And he needs the walk,' she added to me.

'You're afraid to let me be alone with a blonde Amazon?' I asked.

Beth chuckled at me. 'When I let you go off with blonde Amazons,' she said, 'you'll know that I think you've got back enough of your strength to be able to fight them off.'

I thought it over and decided that I had been paid a compliment.

Hannah returned. 'Miss Johnson,' she said formally. The door closed between them.

Miss Johnson was much as Hannah had described her. Her hair, dress and make-up were all skilfully subdued. Under it all, her bone structure was good and sturdy so that her figure just missed being slender and was athletic instead. I could imagine her being the terror of the hockey field. Her features, her jaw in particular, suggested a certain strength of character but she was visibly too tense, almost nervous, to have been from either the police or the Scottish

Office. I got up and led her to a seat on the settee. I saw Beth noticing the small courtesy and drawing her own conclusion, but in fact I found Miss Johnson not so much sexless as unsexy. I could not have pointed to anything wrong with her and yet I could no more have imagined myself making love to her than to one of my aunts.

She arranged herself neatly with her handbag in her lap. We waited patiently to be told what she wanted.

'I've had a terrible job finding you,' she said at last, 'and now that I'm here I'm not sure how to approach you.' Her accent came from somewhere in Greater Glasgow but it was from one of the better neighbourhoods and not obtrusive. 'Would you mind telling me . . . will you be seeing Noel Cochrane again soon?'

Her guess would have been at least as good as mine and I was on the point of saying so when Beth forestalled me. 'Do you have a message for him?' she asked gently.

When Beth answers a question with a question I know that she's up to something. I sat back to await developments. This was more interesting than Girl Loses Boy.

Miss Johnson, now that this much was out, seemed to relax. 'Yes,' she said. 'I do. Can you put me in touch with him?'

Beth looked doubtful. 'He's never very easy to contact,' she said, which had certainly been true in the past and was even truer now. 'He phones sometimes but we never know when we're going to see him. We could certainly pass a message when he does get in touch. But what brings you to us?'

'Everybody knows that Noel keeps a dog somewhere around here, Mrs Cunningham, a dog that he certainly wouldn't abandon. It was just a matter of finding out which kennels. When I saw in the evening paper that your car had been stolen and a dog was missing, I put two and two together.'

'Very clever,' Beth said approvingly. 'Miss Johnson — or can we use your first name?'

The innocent question seemed to disturb Miss Johnson for a fraction of a second. 'Catherine,' she said. 'They call me Kate.'

'Thank you, Kate. Call me Beth, please. Would you like a drink?'

'No. No, thank you.'

'What's the message?' I asked. A faint cloud of annoyance drifted across Beth's face and was gone. For some reason of her own she was pumping Miss Johnson for information which would probably have come of its own accord, I thought, except that Miss Johnson was showing clear signs of preferring to control the twists and turns of discussion.

'I'd rather speak to him myself.'

I decided to play along with Beth. 'I don't see why,' I said.

Miss Johnson's previously smooth brow creased in thought. 'It sounds so secretive and mysterious. But it really is confidential. Tell him,' she said slowly, 'that he must do as he thinks best, but Jake and Simeon have changed sides and Nigel H is going to call on some Glasgow heavies. Noel must get hold of Donald and tell him to give it up and go home at once, and to stay away from the Bothy at all costs. Will you tell him all that? And keep it to yourselves? Please? It really is very important.' She looked at me. I thought that for two pins she would have batted her eyelashes.

Hiding inside her, I was sure, was too powerful and self-assured a lady for her to be convincing in her role of helpless little girl in need of help from the big strong man. Again, I nearly put my foot in it. I was about to say that at least one Donald was already hospitalized, but I caught a glare from Beth, limited to Miss Johnson's blind side, that would have stopped a charging bull.

'I can see that it's important,' Beth said. 'Would you say it again, just to be sure that we've got it right?'

Miss Johnson began to repeat the message, but refused to be drawn by such questions as 'Jake who?'. 'Please pass the message,' she said again. 'Please. Donald doesn't mean any harm and he doesn't know what he's getting himself into.'

'You're very fond of him, aren't you?' Beth said.

Miss Johnson looked coy although under the clever make-up I could see no sign of a blush. 'I don't want to be rude while I'm asking a favour of you,' she said, 'but that really is no concern of anybody but Donald and myself. We have to be discreet,' she added, 'so that there should be no doubt about it.

'He isn't married, is he?' Beth asked in a tone of great concern.

Miss Johnson smiled at last. Her smile sat lopsidedly on her symmetrical mouth. 'No,' she said. 'He's not married. And now I must go. Remember the message, please, please, please.'

I got up to see her out. To my surprise, Beth came with us. With the minimum of farewells Miss Johnson slid into a two-year-old Mazda and drove very carefully away.

We turned back into the house. Beth paused in the hall to note down the number of Miss Johnson's car. 'I think,' she said, 'that I'll give Henry a ring. He may have an idea.'

'I suppose he might. Shouldn't we tell the police?'

'Tell them what?'

'They could trace her car number.'

'They could. But why should they? There are other ways.'

She had stopped making sense. I yawned. 'We ought to have told the poor woman that her boyfriend's in hospital.'

'If he is her boyfriend. But then she wouldn't have given us the message,' Beth pointed out.

'For all the good it did us.'

'Exactly. Anyway, she'll find out in the morning.'

I wanted to ask how she could be so sure, but the usual night-time waves of tiredness were coming over me. I went through to the kitchen to make myself a milky drink.

While I waited for the pan to boil, the phone rang. I delayed in the hope that Beth would take it in the sitting room, but evidently she was again deep in her weepie. I picked it up.

'Are you holding it for him?'

'Am I holding what for who and why do you want to know?' I asked irritably.

'That's all I wanted.' The connection was broken.

I thought that the man had had an accent from somewhere in the Borders, but the conversation had been so brief that I could not be sure.

As I took myself to bed, the taped film must have finished. I could hear Beth talking to Henry on the phone. My mind was too sluggish to take in the words. I flopped into bed. Miss Johnson and the voice on the phone were blurring together in my mind. I zonked out in mid-thought.

Five

My first concern was still for Jove. He was a biddable dog with a soft mouth and a good nose, well on the way to being a stalwart worker. But outside his job in life he had a puppyish, bumbling charm which I found irresistible. Whatever the law might say, I was determined not to stand by and see him shot by some nervous volunteer. At the same time, his continued absence posed a real threat to our livelihood and, if by some terrible mischance he should really be carrying rabies, to human life.

When I managed to relegate Jove to the back of my mind, I found that I was also in a fever of impatience to get my hands on the new car. But Henry had taken his own car home and for once he failed to turn up with Isobel in the morning. 'I've no idea where he's gone,' Isobel said peevishly. 'He got up early, which is unusual for him, and I could hear him making phone-calls. Then he made his own breakfast, which is just as unusual and I hope he hasn't poisoned himself. And then, as I finished getting dressed, he just drove off with a smug expression on his face.'

As it happened, Hugh Morris was equally impatient to obtain delivery of Beech. He was on the phone by ten. I explained that whenever practicable I always insisted on introducing the client and the dog to each other properly and in as near to working conditions as possible. Twenty minutes later Hugh and the new car were on the doorstep.

Together, we spent a happy hour or more at the Moss. None of the quarry on offer was in season, but we managed to simulate some real work using a shotgun and the dummy launcher. Man and dog soon developed an understanding. I could tell that a close relationship would follow in its own time.

Henry was waiting beside his car as we walked up the drive and he signalled that he wanted to confer. I let Daffy drive Hugh and Beech home. It was agony, letting Daffy have first drive of the new car although I knew that she was a far more careful driver than her bizarre appearance would have suggested. The car would return undamaged.

We went into the kitchen. This was where almost every scrap of indoor life was lived during working hours. It was warm and spacious and discussion could involve anyone who was cooking a meal, preparing dog-food or attending to Sam at the time. Also, there was a percolator with coffee always available. We found Beth, as usual trying to cope with Sam's voracious appetite, Isobel dealing with accounts at the scrubbed table, and Hannah preparing puppy mash. Henry and I helped ourselves to coffee and took the two basket chairs.

'You've been busy,' I said to Henry. 'According to Isobel you jumped into your car and drove off furiously in all directions.'

'I didn't say furiously,' Isobel murmured without looking up from her papers. 'Those days are long gone.'

'Irritably, perhaps. And in only one direction,' Henry said. 'So I have been busy. You don't have to make it sound like some ghastly aberration. And now to save you asking, I'm about to tell you what I've been busy at. Beth,' Henry said, leap-frogging clear over his whole story and beginning at the end, 'you turned out to be absolutely right.' He smiled broadly, so that the lines that time had etched in his face dug more deeply.

'That's good,' Beth murmured.

'What was she right about?' I asked patiently.

Henry turned his attention to me. 'Ah. I remember now. When Beth phoned me last night, she said that you'd gone off to bed.

She told me about your visitor and passed on several guesses, frankly admitting that they were no more than just that. Guesses. She suggested that your Miss Johnson was not in fact a Miss Johnson at all but was trying to hide her identity. On the other hand, when asked for a Christian name the lady seemed to be caught flat-footed. She produced Kate or Catherine reluctantly and after a hesitation too brief for selecting another alias. Beth also suggested that she probably worked for Cook and Simpson.'

'What on earth gave you that idea?' I asked Beth.

Beth tried to shrug but was hampered by a double armful of guzzling toddler. 'She said that "everybody" knew that Noel Cochrane kept a dog around here. When someone says "everybody" in that sort of context they don't really mean everybody in the world, they mean everybody in some closed circle. She could have meant the local dog club or some such body, but the workplace seemed more likely.'

'Spot on,' Henry said. 'Beth also suggested that she was probably a secretary, and to somebody senior.'

I nearly asked how Beth could possibly know such a thing but then realized that, compared to Beth's, my eye for a woman's dress hardly began to start to commence.

'That was an office dress she had on,' Beth

explained. 'She was smart but severe, just what a senior executive would want. She would only have to change her dress and let her hair down and she'd be ready to go out on the town. She was a long way above the typing pool.'

'She could have been an executive,' I said.

Beth shook her head at me, pityingly. 'No, if she herself had been at management level she would have splashed out rather more and in a less disciplined way; and if she'd been a biochemist or something like that she wouldn't have bothered to be so smart for work, where she'd have worn a lab coat. From her clothes and her car, she wasn't short of a bob or two, which again suggested seniority — or a rich father or boyfriend.'

'Or maybe all three,' said Hannah. 'Lucky bitch!' She sniffed and went back to her feeding bowls.

'Be that as it may,' Henry said firmly, 'it was easy to follow her up. I phoned a friendly policeman who checked out the car's number for me. It's registered to a Miss Catherine Otterburn at an address not too far from Cook and Simpson's Glasgow plant.

'So I phoned the plant and asked for Kate Otterburn. A voice which didn't realize just how much it was telling me said that she wasn't available this morning but that I could be connected with the temp who was looking after the managing director for the moment.'

'Being interviewed by the fuzz,' Beth said wisely. 'I phoned for Inspector Tirrell after I spoke to you last night, Henry. He'd gone home but I left a message with his sergeant suggesting more or less what I'd suggested to you.'

'You may well be right,' Henry said. 'Or she may be unavailable for any one of a number of other reasons.' (As Henry spoke, I realized that he was avoiding saying aloud that Miss Otterburn might by now be another corpse in the countryside.) 'Rather than stir anything up, I said that I'd call back later. But before I rang off I asked for the MD's name and was told that it was Heatherington. Nigel Heatherington.'

'Nigel H,' said Beth, 'who was hiring some heavies.' She had managed to satisfy Sam's appetite for the moment and was nursing his somnolent body.

'So,' Henry said, 'I phoned an old friend who had at one time been a director of Cook and Simpson. He called me back a little later. He had been in touch with Miss Otterburn's predecessor, one Madge Laidlaw now living in retirement near Perth, and she was willing to grant me an interview. So that's the direction in which I drove sanely off.

'The lady was valuable, not only for her intimate knowledge of the company but because she had a considerable chip on her shoulder. Being no chicken, she had been pushed into retirement, she assured me, so that somebody younger, prettier and probably more liberal with her favours could be appointed in her place. Whether that was the truth or just a slighted lady's imagination working overtime I know not. But she gave me the lowdown on the company structure and personnel.

'The company specializes in veterinary products and carries out a great deal of research, but I already knew that. They confine their research and manufacturing activities to Scotland because we are less troubled by the activities of the animal rights activists up here; and they divide their work between Glasgow and Aberdeen to make industrial espionage more difficult. Broadly, basic materials are produced in a plant between Aberdeen and Fraserburgh. Then, using code numbers only, they're blended, finished and packaged in Glasgow where most of the management and some of the research is based. They sell worldwide.

'As I'd already discovered for myself, Nigel H is Nigel Heatherington, the managing director and, according to his former secretary, a forceful, ruthless man — although few men in their own lifetimes could live down to her image of him. He's a member of the original Simpson family and himself a major shareholder, so he carries a good deal of clout. Jake must be Jake Spurway, who is nominally one of the security men but is widely rumoured to be Mr Heatherington's personal fixer and general tough. According to Miss Laidlaw, Spurway and his assistant, by name Spragg, are or were occasional drinking companions of Noel Cochrane — for whatever that's worth.

'Cochrane, as we know, started off as a biochemist but moved over into sales. She heard that he had been brought back from India to become head of the publicity and marketing department when the two were rolled together comparatively recently, but that merger had happened since her retirement so she had no details to give me. The only Donald she could call to mind in that area of the company is Donald Aggleton, Noel's assistant and right hand, and her description of that young man, allowing for a slight leaning towards the romantic, accords with the lad we found yesterday.'

Hannah was ready with the meal for the younger pups. She loaded the trolley but paused. 'What about the dead woman?' she said. 'The one I had to identify.'

'I tried the description you gave us on Miss Laidlaw. Assuming that she was a member of that circle,' Henry said, 'she would have to be Harriet Williams, Cochrane's colleague heading the PR side of the department. That would seem to be a rather rash assumption, except that Miss Laidlaw coyly revealed that there had been a romantic attachment between Miss Williams and Donald Aggleton.'

Beth was frowning. 'But Miss Otterburn seemed to be suggesting that any romance was between Donald Aggleton and herself.'

'That,' Henry pointed out, 'was while she was calling herself Johnson. It may have been Lies for a Prize Day.'

'It certainly gets more and more difficult to guess who might be in league with who,' I said.

Henry nodded sadly. 'That's almost all that I got from the lady, although she said not to hesitate before phoning her if we have any more questions. But my friend had given me one more snippet of information. He said that he sold out his shares in Cook and Simpson on a vague hint from a pal — which may have had some substance in it, because the shares have fallen substantially during the past week. I asked Miss Laidlaw about this. She knew nothing about share movements, she said, any money she had was safely tucked away in a building society, but at the time of her retirement there had already been rumours of a major disagreement at management level. There had been raised voices behind closed doors and memos sealed in envelopes marked "Confidential" which had never been put out for filing.'

'Wow!' said Hannah. 'I'd better go,' she added reluctantly.

I felt a prickle of conscience. 'Do you need help?' I asked.

'You're busy. Daffy'll be back in a minute. She can help me.' Resolutely turning her back on all the excitement, Hannah pushed the squeaking trolley out into the passage.

'If Mr Heatherington has his own personal tough guy,' Beth said, 'why is he said to be hiring Glasgow heavies?'

'Because Jake went solo, according to Miss Otterburn,' Henry reminded her. 'Of course, both those snippets were disgorged on an occasion when not a word was uttered which has since been shown to be true. On the other hand, the lady may have been sailing under false colours but nobody can fib all the time. Isobel, you might be able to find out some more about Cook and Simpson on the Old Vet Network.'

Isobel humphed. 'Vets are the last people they'd allow to see their dirty laundry.'

It seemed to me that the whole thing was getting out of hand. 'Do we really need to do all this investigation?' I demanded. 'It may make an interesting pastime — as if

time didn't pass all too quickly already —
but it's police business, not ours. We've got
my gun back. If we can recover Jove un-
hurt . . .'

'In my opinion,' Henry said, 'yes, you do
need to help things along. You may need
friends in the police, and if there's a song
and dance about Jove escaping from custody
it may stand you in good stead if you can
show that he went missing as a by-product
of some much bigger machinations.'

Reluctantly, I saw that there was something in his point of view.

There came the sound of an engine and
the brush of tyres on our gravel. I craned
my neck. As best I could see, the new car
had no dents in it. Daffy looked in, gave me
a thumbs-up signal and went off to help
Hannah.

The phones rang. The cordless was beside
me, so I answered.

'Mr Cunningham?' It was a gruff voice
with a broad accent. 'This is Bruce Henry
at Mannofield Farm by Kindore. I hear
you've lost a dog.'

'I have indeed,' I said.

'Well, there's a black Lab been running
wild near here.'

'Where was he last seen?' My voice went
up so that the others all stared at me.

'In the trees at the western march, down
by the firth.'

'Do nothing,' I said. 'I'm on my way. For the love of God don't call the police just yet.'

'O'er late for that,' Mr Henry said cheerfully. 'My neighbour, Mr Tom McLoan, ca'd them an hour back. He thought to call me about it and I minded that you'd put the word about. And there was mention of a bittie siller?'

'If that's the dog and I get him back safe, you'll get the reward.' I pushed the phone at Beth. 'Black Lab seen at Kindore,' I said. 'Coming, Henry?'

'Kindore's rather far from where the crates were found,' Beth protested. 'It must be fifteen miles.'

'Twelve at the most. And there's no saying how far a dog can wander when it's lost and trying to find its way home,' I pointed out.

Henry was already on his feet. 'Where would Jove think of as home, after all this time?' he asked.

'Here, probably,' I said. 'But if so, Kindore's in the wrong direction. If he's making for India he's got a long swim in front of him.'

'You always said that Jove was the strongest swimmer you'd ever trained,' Beth said.

Into the back of the new estate car went a travelling box, heavy gloves and the tranquillizer dart-gun with its bag of accessories. Henry got into the passenger seat and we moved off.

Half a mile up the road, we came to a halt. I had forgotten the anti-theft precaution installed by the previous owner. Fizzing with impatience, because at any moment some trigger-happy volunteer might be inscribing Jove's name on a bullet, I cursed myself aloud, pressed the switch and ground the starter until the pump refilled the carburettor and the engine fired.

'If it stops you, it'll stop a thief,' Henry said soothingly as we got moving again.

I stopped muttering to myself and let the comment hang, concentrating on hustling the unfamiliar car over familiar roads. There was a new feeling of tautness and a silence where the old car had clattered.

My function as the prime trainer and supplier of gundogs for the area had earned me a lot of invitations to shoot or pick up and I had also visited much of the shore of the Tay on wildfowling trips. From Kindore I had no difficulty finding Mannofield Farm, but the farmhouse and yard were in clear view from the minor road serving them and there was neither activity nor an unusual number of vehicles to be seen. If Mr McLoan at . . . I searched my memory and came up with the name Knock Farm. If Mr McLoan had made the original report to the police,

Knock Farm was where the action would begin.

The farm road to Knock Farm was roughly where I remembered it. Vehicles, mostly olive-green, were parked short of the farmyard and a dozen or more roughly-dressed men in wellingtons were milling around the grey stone buildings. Apart from the complete absence of dogs it looked too much like the prelude to a shoot for my liking, and indeed some of the men had bagged guns slung over their shoulders. I drew up behind the last vehicle. Beyond the farmhouse I could see the Tay, a broad river but much narrower than its width twenty miles nearer the sea. From the stir over the sandbanks the tide was running out fast, flashing and sparkling in the sunshine of another fine spring day.

To my partial relief I found Inspector Tirrell there, newly arrived on the scene but about to take charge. He seemed as relieved to see me and even wore a hesitant smile as he came to meet us. 'I phoned and spoke to Mrs Cunningham,' he said, 'but you were already on the road. I thought you'd want to be along.'

'Damn right I'd want to be along,' I said. I raised my voice so that I was addressing the throng. 'Let's be clear about this. The dog was stolen out of quarantine but there's no reason whatever to suppose that he has rabies. In fact he's been thoroughly vaccinated against it.'

'Vaccination isn't a hundred per cent,' said a man. I recognized him suddenly as an SSPCA inspector, Thane by name. I thought that he could be trouble.

'Damn near it,' I said.

He shook his head. He was a skinny man with pop-eyes and in the past I had found him both officious and inclined to see mischief where none existed. 'There's a doubt been cast on the effectiveness of it. I saw an article about it just last week.'

'There's still no reason to believe that the dog is infected,' I retorted. 'Anyway, he knows me and I have a tranquillizer gun here. I'll be glad of help to find him, but after that I'll make the first approach, so that if anybody gets bitten it'll be me. All we're required to do is to get the dog back into quarantine. Let me make it absolutely clear that anyone unnecessarily shooting a valuable trained dog will certainly be sued for damages by a loving owner.' *If the loving owner ever shows his face again,* I added to myself.

Several of the men were nodding agreement. I recognized two keepers and some members of the local wildfowling club. They knew the value of a good dog. I had also attended a public meeting at which several of them had argued cogently against the outdated quarantine regulations. I began to feel more hopeful.

A thick-set figure turned away from a huge, black, Japanese four-wheel-drive and turned a face towards me which reminded me irresistibly of a male salmon ready to mate — coloured and with a distinct hook to the jaw. A hat adorned with fishing flies was pulled down over the brow but I had no difficulty recognizing Hector Tholess, my least favourite politician, MP for some-where-or-other in the central belt and for-mer cabinet minister, done up in a tweed plus-four suit with highly polished boots and gaiters. I had never liked his politics or the image he presented during his many appearances on television; and when he had turned up as a fellow guest on a shoot my dislike had increased. I saw that he was a greedy shot, self-assertive to the point of being dangerous and, worst of all, incon-siderate to his dog. He had, I remembered, an estate near Perth and I recognized at least one of the men present as being on his staff.

'Rabies is not something to take chances with,' Tholess said in a tone which brooked no argument.

'Nobody is suggesting taking chances,' I said with what I hoped was equal authority. 'The dog is healthy. But even if he had rabies, which he doesn't, and even if he then bit one of you, which he won't, there would still be plenty of time for protective shots.'

'Which Mr Thane tells us are less than a hundred per cent effective.' As he spoke, Tholess was unbagging a deer rifle with an expensive telescopic sight and feeding it with what looked like .243 cartridges. 'And what is the first symptom? Untypical behaviour, that's what! And how do you know what's untypical?'

The question was clearly intended to be rhetorical but Thane answered for him. 'In the wild, one symptom is when an animal which would normally run away comes towards you.'

'Exactly. I'll tell you this, if that dog comes towards me, it's dead.'

'And how will you know if it's the right dog?' Henry asked.

Tholess transferred his black glare from me to Henry. 'Right or wrong, mad or no. Any black dog approaching me this morning has to be mad,' he added with grim humour.

I turned to Tirrell. 'The dog knows me well,' I said. 'He'll come to me. Make sure that I get a chance to collect him unharmed. Could you delay the start while I seek an interdict to restrain the honourable but trigger-happy gentleman?'

Tholess made a noise which Henry later

described as resembling a dinosaur's fart but failed to come up with a timely riposte.

Tirrell shook his head. He was looking unhappy. 'I have my orders,' he said.

'If they include an order to shoot the dog without attempting a safe recapture,' Henry said, 'give me the name of the person issuing that order. It will come in useful when the writs begin to fly. Failing which, the writs will have your name on the front.'

'We'll give you your chance,' Tirrell said to me.

'I'll need my crate for transportation,' I told him. 'To satisfy the law not myself.'

'You can have it. It's behind the police garage at Cupar.'

I handed my car keys to Henry. He looked relieved. He is past the age at which long walks start to exact a toll in aches and pains. I took the travelling box, the gloves and the dart-gun out of the back of the car. 'Meet us back here,' I told Henry.

'No problem. If the crate fits into the car.'

'It will,' I said. 'Definitely. If it doesn't, come straight back.'

He sat in the driver's seat and started the engine. He was half-way back to the road before I thought of reminding him to press the special switch. Well, that was two of us who would not forget again.

I stowed the box for the moment in the back of Tirrell's Range Rover and, while he developed his plan of action with the help of a couple of locals, I busied myself readying three darts with what I considered to be appropriate doses of tranquillizer. The one that I loaded into the dart-gun would have stunned Tholess, let alone a Labrador.

Tirrell's plan was simple. The line could spread wide apart as we crossed the fields as long as each hedge and ditch was covered. Thane, the SSPCA man, was not carrying a gun. As we set off, a man in jeans and a sweater with a mean face, who I recognized belatedly as Mr McLoan, was threatening dire reprisals on anyone who traversed his crops by any other than the tramlines left by the tractor.

I placed myself not far from Tholess in the line. If he lifted his rifle against any dog that I thought might be Jove, I would fell him with a dart first and apologize for a regrettable accident, caused by a stumble over a stone, after he came round.

Two fields on, we came to a patch of rough ground, a place of weeds and boulders, where I remembered a wounded goose once planing down into cover and being fetched out by Samson and here the line had to close up. Further on, we entered a long strip of trees. Because of a deep gulley, the place was fenced against cattle and densely undergrown. The older men crossed the fields while the rest of us cursed and sweated through the trees, treading down the brambles and prodding sticks into bushes. There was some excitement when a large fox was put out of cover but no shot was fired. No instructions had been given about foxes and nobody was sure whether they were on the day's quarry list along with black Labradors.

The stream, and the gulley and tree-strip with it, made a right-angle turn towards the Tay. We had a rest while some of the older men made the long trip through a pasture and around the outside of the angle. A compact flock of sheep trotted ahead of them. There were midges under the trees, unseasonably early so that I for one had not thought to bring insect repellent. Several of us drifted to the fence in the hope of getting a respite for our ears and foreheads. Some of the men lit pipes or cigarettes and the smoke helped to drive the little pests away.

Trying to keep Tholess within range, I found, had brought me near the SSPCA man. I pointed the dart-gun into the ground. I had a feeling that somewhere there was a question I should be asking him. 'What did you mean about the vaccinations losing their effectiveness?' I asked.

'Exactly that. These things happen. Mutations produce new strains and then, of course, the scientists have to go back to work.'

'With the use of animal testing?' I asked mischievously.

His face clouded. 'I'm afraid so. We can't prevent it, wouldn't if we could. The most we can do is to try and ensure that it's done as mercifully as possible and press for more humane methods to be found. There's no adequate alternative yet. You'd think there would be. They grow the diploid cells, which are the basis of the vaccine, in human tissue culture but apparently that doesn't work for testing. Then again, the efficacy of some types of diploid cell vaccine can be drastically reduced if the patient's taking chloraquin for malaria.'

'You're very well informed,' I said. 'I'm impressed.'

He hesitated and then decided to be modest. 'Three weeks ago I wouldn't have known any of this. It was all in that article. I was interested . . .'

'I can see that you would be.' Something was stirring at the back of my mind. 'Would any of this explain why the Cook and Simpson shares have been taking a knock?'

He thought it over, his pop-eyes staring over my shoulder. 'I suppose it might. But they'll take a damned sight bigger knock if the company starts getting lawsuits from widows.' He spoke with a relish that I found distasteful.

The line was ready to move again shortly after that. We resumed our places and the midges came back to the attack.

We were moving downhill now and the going was slightly easier. From memory, I thought that we were close to the boundary ('the march') between the two farms and therefore nearing where the dog had been seen. Through gaps in the tree canopy I could see the water. A small boat powered by an outboard motor was puttering across the tide. The two men in it were trolling for salmon.

The line moved slowly, with many pauses while somebody negotiated a particularly sticky bit of cover or investigated some possible hiding place under upturned roots or piles of cut branches. I was beginning to think that we had drawn a blank and that our quarry had moved on.

A steep bank rose from high-water mark and there the trees and fences came to an end. It was a place where I had once been landed by boat before dawn to lie in wait for the geese. Slightly nearer to me I could see the brick structure with a concrete roof behind which I had lurked, close to the stream. It was about the size of an ordinary bathroom and I guessed that it had once held a waterpump before mains water had come to the farm. It was on my side of the stream and gulley and the doorless opening faced my way, but it was the man on the other side of the gulley who said, in a throaty voice, 'There's something in there. I saw it move.'

I stopped. The other men closed in slowly. The tension seemed enough to drown out all sounds except for several clicks as of guns being closed or safety catches slipped off. Tholess pushed forward. I let the muzzle of the dart-gun stray in his direction as if out of carelessness and he froze. I wondered what the penalty would be for tranquillizing a member of parliament against his will. A CBE at the very least.

'Everybody hold it,' Tirrell said sharply. He nodded to me. Tholess made an impatient noise.

I had been blowing occasional trills on my silent whistle and I tried it again. There was a small sound in reply but no friendly form came out, tail-wagging fit to bowl himself over. When I moved forward again I heard a rumble from beyond the doorway.

I had never heard Jove growl. It would be very unlike him to growl at me. Nor was this how I would have expected Jove's growl to sound. But, as Tholess had said, one of the first symptoms of the onset of rabies is unnatural behaviour. I sent up a silent prayer that if my sphincter let me down it would do so discreetly and in silence.

A tranquillizer dart works quickly but not instantaneously. My mouth had gone dry and something was wandering on my spine although I could not have said whether it was making its way up or down. I thought of borrowing one of the shotguns and going in with a shotgun in one hand and the dart-gun in the other, but that would be a slow and cumbersome defence at close range. Instead, I replaced the dart with one more lightly loaded. It might not have stopped a rampant politician in his tracks but it would put a Labrador to sleep in a hurry.

I leaned my back against the brickwork, out of the sight of whatever might be inside, and spoke very softly. 'Get ready,' I said. 'I'm going in. If I come out again in a hell of a hurry, be ready to shoot. But be sure and let me get out of the way first.'

The curve of faces nodded in unison.

I stepped into the doorway. 'Jove?' I said.

It was dark inside the brick structure and made darker by my occupying the doorway, but I was in no hurry to step in and to the side. The rumbling rose to a snarl that set the hair crawling up the back of my neck, but the dark shape crouching tensely in the far corner kept its distance.

My eyes began to adjust to the poor light. I squatted down, still ready to hurl myself backwards. The move allowed more light in and at the same time would have made me look less threatening. After a long moment, still crouched, I backed out of the door.

The SSPCA man was nearby and I spoke to him. 'This is one for you,' I said. 'I seem to remember someone advertising for a lost black Labrador bitch three or four weeks ago.'

'She's in there?'

'There's a bitch in there,' I said. 'She's certainly black and mostly Labrador and she's got a litter of pups. She's as thin as a rake, poor thing, after feeding them and living off what she could pick up on the foreshore. I can tranquillize her for you if you like.'

He shook his head. 'Leave it to me,' he said. 'That took some guts,' he added grudgingly.

I thought that Beth would probably say it took a hell of a lot of stupidity. But I had believed that it was Jove in there and I was sure that Jove would never bite me and almost as sure that he was clear of rabies. That sort of certainty may be the death of me some day.

As we walked back to the cars I stayed as far as I could from Hector Tholess and fell into casual conversation with a man whose face was vaguely familiar to me. When he said that he was the water bailiff, my interest quickened. A word that Miss Johnson had used had been slipping in and out of my mind. 'What do you understand by the word "bothy"?' I asked him.

'Well, now,' he said. 'It used to mean a rough sort of place for farmworkers to bide in, but there's precious few farmworkers any more and the few there are expect council house standards or better. Nowadays, it mostly means a fishing hut. Sometimes just a wee shed where anglers can leave their gear, shelter from the rain or brew a pot of tea; but I've heard the word used of some smart wee places where a man could spend a week and maybe entertain a friend as well.'

'That's what I thought,' I said. 'Are there many along this side of the Tay?'

'There's a few,' he admitted.

Hugh Morris had kindly left a road map of the locality in the car. It was an advertising hand-out but I appreciated the thought. 'Could you mark them on a map?' I asked.

'I'm not saying I ken them a',' he said cautiously. 'I ken the most of them but that's only along my beat of the river. I'll do what I can.'

Henry was waiting with the car complete with crate, which I was relieved to note was as neat a fit in the new car as it had been in the old one. While my new friend made pencil marks on the map and Henry had a word with the Inspector, I unloaded the dart-gun and recovered the travelling box from Tirrell's car.

'There's no word of any more cars having been stolen,' Henry said when he rejoined me.

It was dawning on me that we had missed lunch and suddenly I was ravenously hungry. I knew of a small hotel not too far away which kept the bar open during the afternoon and served snacks whenever they were wanted. Henry, whose appetite of all his faculties was the least damaged by age, took very little persuading.

Six

The hotel was little more than a pub with a couple of bedrooms for visitors. It had existed, at least for the past hundred years, without paying any attention to changing fashions. It was still a place of dark-stained pitch-pine linings, enamelled wallpaper, battleship-quality linoleum and bentwood chairs and tables.

This absolute refusal to upgrade the amenities was balanced by a similar refusal to lower the standard of the food, which was in the best tradition of Scots cooking and was prepared and served by the landlord's wife at almost any hour. The sole concession to change had been to interpret the liberalization of the licensing laws as a permit to open and close whenever the whim took them or the customers demanded.

We waited in the empty bar for our stovies — a peculiarly Scottish dish of potatoes stewed in onions. Henry bought beer for us both and brought it to a table. I gave him the story of the morning with very little expurgation and then we sat and sipped in companionable silence. I was still winding down after the earlier surge of adrenalin when I had half expected to be rushed at by a rabid Labrador.

Somebody else knew of the place, because a large car, a recent model but battered and already beginning to rust, pulled in beside mine and a smooth-faced man got out. I was sure that I had seen him among the walking searchers but, if so, then he had managed an almost complete change of outer clothing. He had been dressed earlier in jeans and wellingtons, but now he had on a business suit, polished shoes and a tie that could have belonged to some school, club or regiment, although I was unable to identify it. With the tweed cap put aside, his black hair was neat.

'Do you suppose,' I asked Henry, 'that Noel Cochrane has Jove with him?'

'I doubt it,' Henry said after a moment. 'Even if he'd managed to find him, or to make contact with whoever had him, I don't see that that would do him any good. He couldn't take him abroad secretly, except perhaps by yacht. In this country, Jove would be as bad as a visiting card. And if he does have him,' Henry said, 'Noel becomes the most likely suspect for having knocked Donald Something on the head.'

'If Noel was already planning to vanish abroad and had an alternative passport in his pocket,' I said, 'he might well be able to take Jove with him. Nobody gives much of a damn about outward bound dogs. Apart from our paranoia about quarantine, travelling within the EC has become much easier. Maybe they're already abroad. In which case, all the fuss and flapdoodle will go on for ever.'

'Nothing lasts for ever,' Henry said. 'Aeons and aeons, but not for ever. Work on the assumption that they're still around.'

'So, apart from trying to be in at the recovery of Jove, do we leave it all to the police?' I asked.

'It still seems to me,' Henry said slowly, 'that you need a result. One trouble with the police is that some of them are more interested in closing a file than in arriving at the truth. As things stand, on the face of it, you've let a quarantined animal get away from you. If your last hypothesis was correct, it might even look as though you let the owner walk off with him. While Jove's on the loose, there's the added possibility that he might develop rabies, bite somebody, start an epidemic, you name it. If you — we — get him back safely, a different light is shed. Somebody tried to make off with the dog but failed. You follow me?'

The smooth-faced man came into the bar. The landlord appeared and served him with a whisky. Then, instead of the customary nod and a mention of the weather before retiring to another table in the opposite corner of the room, the man crossed the floor, put his whisky down between our beers and said, 'Do you mind if I join you?' He had a gentle voice out of keeping with the intensity of his expression and no trace of an accent.

'We don't so much mind,' Henry said, 'as wonder why you should want to.'

The man chuckled as though Henry had cracked the funniest joke in history. Then he looked at me. 'Captain Cunning-ham . . . ?'

'Mister Cunningham,' I said.

'Mister, then. I'm Michael Coutts. I want to get in touch with your friend Noel Coch-rane.'

I was about to point out that Noel Cochrane wasn't a friend of mine when the thought came to me that he probably was.

'You and everybody else,' Henry said.

'That does seem to be so. But I, for one, do not mean him any harm and it could be very much to his advantage that I get to him before any of the other parties.'

'Well, I can't help you,' I said. 'I don't know where he is. I wish to God I did.'

'Is that really so?' He seemed to be asking himself the question rather than expressing doubt to me. 'Tell me, when did you see him last?'

'One moment,' Henry said firmly. 'Just what is your locus in this?'

'I beg your pardon?' Coutts said. This time his question was expressing huffiness. It struck me as calculated or even practised. Without being quite sure where the thought came from, I was beginning to think that he was a bit of an actor if not a poseur. He had changed his clothes so that he would fit in with his company of the moment and he seemed able to produce whatever manner suited his purpose.

Henry, I could see, was thinking along the same lines. 'I mean,' he said firmly, 'are you representing the police, the family, the local authority or the media? Or, of course, the dog?'

'I've already told you that I'm a friend of his.'

This was getting a bit much. 'No, you haven't,' I said. 'You hinted at it.'

Coutts thought it over. 'I believe you're right,' he said. 'Well, if I forgot to mention it, I truly am friendly with Noel, to the extent that we've often had a friendly drink together after work. And I genuinely am concerned for him.'

'All of which may be perfectly true,' said Henry, 'but you're still a member of the press. I've known that from the moment you arrived, I've just been waiting to find out how long it would take you to reveal yourself.'

Coutts hesitated and then nodded. 'How did you know?' he asked.

'Even if I hadn't recognized your byline, I can see the press sticker on your car from here.'

I craned my neck. There was certainly a sticker on Coutts's windscreen. Henry could see it from a more favourable angle than I could. I took another and more curious look at Coutts. He was unlike the common run of journalists. For one thing, he was neatly but inconspicuously dressed, well shaved and, even after our walk across country, his nails were clean and unbroken. I would have put him down as a modestly successful businessman, which I suppose in a way he was.

Our meal arrived then. The landlord's wife looked at Michael Coutts enquiringly. He shook his head but asked for another whisky. When she had served him and left he said, 'Perhaps I should have been more open with you, but some people are wary of speaking openly to the papers. If you know my stuff you know that I'm not gutter press.'

'As I recall, you come closer to what they call investigative journalism,' Henry said. 'Although just what kind of journalism isn't investigative beats me.'

'The kind that makes it up as it goes along,' I said.

'Which is not my style at all,' Coutts said. His manner was persuasive. 'So I'll come clean. As I told you, Noel and I use the same pub and we get along well. That, I suppose, is why he picked on me and not some other hack. Anyway, about a week ago he phoned me at the office and asked me to meet him that evening in the usual place. When I turned up, I could see that he was on edge. He told me that he might have what he described as "one hell of a story" for me. He wanted to be sure that he could get hold of me at short notice and he noted down places and phone numbers where I might be reached.

'He also said that it went against all he'd ever learned, to blow the gaff on somebody he owed so much, but there came a time when enough was enough. I think those were his words. Of course, he was mildly sloshed at the time.'

'And he didn't drop a hint as to whether he was talking about his employers?'

'My guess is that he was,' Coutts said. 'Then, the day before yesterday, he phoned me on my mobile to come and meet him at Prestwick Airport. He'd hand me the whole thing on a plate. And he didn't want any money for it, which makes him unique among informants. But he never turned up. There was a message at my office to say that he'd be in touch. And that was all.'

'Yet you arrived here,' Henry said.

'Nothing else is breaking just now. I knew that Noel's dog was in quarantine near here, so when a stringer phoned in about cars being stolen, one of them containing a dog, and a woman's body being found, it seemed that this had to be where the action was. Even if the mention of a dog was purest coincidence, there would still be a story of sorts. I came hotfoot.'

'I expect you did,' said Henry. 'But the temperature of your feet is not at issue. How do we know that you're on Mr Cochrane's side and not planning a hatchet job, some terrible exposé?'

'Exposé of what?' Coutts asked.

'I don't know of what,' Henry said irritably. 'I'd be grateful if you could tell me. But half the human race have secrets they'd rather not see plastered across the front pages. Present company excepted, of course.'

'Personally I'd put it higher than fifty per cent,' Coutts said thoughtfully, 'and not except anybody, but my experience tends to be selective. I've no evidence to offer you of my good intentions — nothing, at least, that would stand up in court. I can only tell you in all honesty that it was he who first approached me, that I believe that any present difficulties he may be facing are related to whatever he planned to divulge and that once those facts are out in the open any danger will be lifted. That, I find, is very often the case. There is no point in pressuring an informant who has already spilled the beans; and revenge seldom pays dividends.'

Henry, looking thoughtful, leaned back in his chair. 'In other words, powerful forces are determined to prevent him speaking to the press.'

Coutts nodded. 'Or are trying to recover evidence. Either way, I would be amazed if it didn't concern some dirty dealings at Cook and Simpson.'

'And you're satisfied that Mr Cochrane, like yourself, is on the side of the angels?' Henry asked.

Coutts looked surprised. 'Yes,' he said, 'I am. The signs are that he's in possession of facts or documents which the firm wants to recover. In theory, I suppose, Noel could be stealing secrets or attempting blackmail; but in neither eventuality would he talk to me.'

'He might threaten to talk to you,' Henry said. 'If he had blackmail in mind, the interested enquiries of a well-known jour-nalist might add a great deal of point to the threats and urgency to the victim's deliberations.'

'We seem to be spending a lot of time making guesses about what Noel may have been thinking. Are motives so important?' I asked. I was far more concerned with how the outcome might affect Noel, Jove and our business.

'Yes,' Henry said slowly, 'I think they are. Always. Look at it this way. Suppose that you'd been in Hungerford when Michael Ryan started shooting up the place. Suppose that, after he'd killed his third or fourth victim, you shot him dead. You'd be a hero?'

'I suppose so,' I said. 'Where is this leading?'

'To this point. Suppose it then came out that you had a grudge against Ryan or something to gain from his death. Perhaps you didn't even know at the time that he'd shot anybody. You see what I'm getting at? Same deed but on the one hand you're in line for a medal and on the other you're wide open to prosecution.'

'That, of course, is true. I honestly believe that Noel's up on a white horse but my mind's at least half open.' Coutts paused and swallowed. 'I also believe that I could go a sandwich after all,' he said. 'I'm not used to long walks in the fresh air. Can I offer you another round?'

'We'd rather keep our wits about us,' Henry said.

'Very wise,' Coutts said. He looked at me curiously. 'Did you have your wits about you this morning? Walking into the den of a possibly rabid dog struck me as being about as witless as you can get.'

'Jove's fully protected by vaccinations,' I protested.

'I wouldn't put too much faith in vaccinations if I were you,' Coutts retorted, almost echoing Mr Thane and the unpleasant Hector Tholess.

'Did he really do that?' Henry asked Coutts but raising his eyebrows at me.

'Don't you go telling Beth,' I said.

Coutts got up and went to the bar. I started to speak again but Henry raised a hand for silence. Coutts was speaking to the landlord and paying us no attention, so I concluded that Henry wanted peace in which to do his thinking.

Coutts returned, not with a sandwich but with another plate of stovies. He may have taken Henry's words to heart, because instead of another whisky he carried a large mug of coffee. 'Well?' he said.

'First of all,' Henry said, 'do you have any identification? For all we know, you may not be from the press at all; worse still, you could be from some tabloid rag and hell-bent on making scandal.'

'Admirably cautious,' Coutts said. From his wallet he produced and gave Henry a card which I took for a credit card, but I could see a miniature photograph bonded to it.

Henry took one look and returned it. 'Very well,' he said. 'You're Michael Coutts. Secondly . . . I'm choosing my words because whatever Noel said to you, he did not state categorically that he was going to give you his story, he said that he "might" have a story for you. He may now be trying to prevent a story rather than make one. On the other hand, he may be dead, injured or liable to arrest, we just don't know. So I'll put it this way. Will you promise to give us fair treatment in anything you write if we, for our part, promise to fill in for you any details that we know and you don't —' Henry paused and drew a deep breath '— with regard to any story which is breaking or which Noel would want to break or which seems to be in the public interest to break?'

My mind had stalled half-way through Henry's interminable question but Coutts took only a few seconds to parse it and come to a decision. 'I can do that,' he said. 'I'm not interested in reporting incidents along the way, only in being able to write up an exclusive, major story when the time comes. But what about the present status quo? I don't want to report it, but I need to know it in order to pursue my own line.'

'Point taken,' said Henry. 'You're an investigator. We want the facts out in the light of day. We'll consider spilling what we know so far if you'll do the same.'

Coutts smiled. 'That seems reasonable.'

'You go first,' Henry said.

Coutts hesitated and then agreed. It was soon as clear to me as it had been to him that he had less to lose than he had to gain. He had made full use of his sources and those of his paper, particularly within the police and ambulance services. Whatever we told the police seemed to have lost little time reaching Mr Coutts. He was able to confirm that the other enquiry after the location of Noel's mobile phone had been from Cook and Simpson. He had tracked down Noel's travel agent; Noel had not booked for California but for Spain, which raised fresh doubts in my mind.

Henry left me to fill in any gaps in Coutts's knowledge. Coutts listened intently and asked a hundred and one questions. He was particularly interested in what we had thought of Catherine Otterburn (alias Johnson) and I tried to recall my impressions of a visitor who had called while I was tired and distracted by worry. 'I put her down as tougher than she acted,' I finished. 'She played the worried girlfriend, but her face showed too much character for a secondary role and her body language was all confidence. I felt that any boyfriend of hers would do the worrying.' During my army service I had often been consulted by squaddies whose wives or girlfriends were playing fast and loose or by ladies asserting that they had been wronged and their hearts broken by one or other of my men, and I had soon learned to distinguish between the gold-diggers and the genuinely wronged.

I was still trying to explain this when we were interrupted. The phone in Henry's pocket began to bleep. Henry looked at me in surprise as he took it out. The phone was in his pocket for no other purpose than to enable him to summon help in case of illness and was seldom used for anything else. I took it from him.

Beth was on the line, speaking very quickly, which with her was usually a sign that she was over the moon and yet I thought that I could detect apprehension in her voice. 'I'm so glad I've found you. Where are you? In some pub?'

'Having a very late lunch at the Ferryden Inn,' I told her. 'The dog wasn't Jove. I think it was the bitch somebody was advertising for a few weeks ago. You remember, you read it out to me. She has a litter with her now. What's happened?'

For once, even the news of a litter failed

to divert Beth. 'You'd better come home straight away. Everything's more or less under control but we've had visitors. I don't want to say any more, especially over the airwaves. Just come. Quickly. Please.'

I could see that Henry and Coutts had been able to follow at least the gist of what she had said. Henry was nodding violently. 'Coming straight away,' I told Beth.

Coutts pushed away the uneaten part of his lunch. 'I'll follow you, if I may,' he said. 'We haven't finished our little chat.'

Even had we wanted to leave him behind it would have been difficult to do so without violence. We left the correct money on the table and hurried out to the cars.

For the third car in succession, I had promised myself to give the new acquisition a gentle introduction to life with the Cunninghams, but Beth's summons seemed to outweigh my good intentions. I put my foot down hard and the car responded to my urging with far less complaint than the old one would have made. Less than ten minutes later I squeezed past a badly parked Jaguar, through the gateway of Three Oaks and followed the short gravel drive, between slightly whiskery lawns and occasional beds of flowers much ravaged by puppies, to the front door. Michael Coutts had been in my mirror all the way.

Beth, Daffy, Hannah and a host of young spaniels were waiting for us, grouped before the sunlit house as if for a photograph. Except for the spaniels, the general mood seemed to be indignation mixed with triumph and spiced with guilt. Any attempt to introduce Michael Coutts or to warn of the presence of the press was doomed. When we asked what the fuss was about, our words seemed to uncork a deluge of verbosity. Each seemed determined to tell the story. Even Sam, secured in his pushchair, was trying to give us the benefit of his own version and, in fact, his exposition was hardly less lucid than the point and counterpoint of the others. The pups for once were too busy foraging around an overturned stainless steel bucket to pay us more than token attention.

The chorus, with allowance for the facts that there were very few pauses for breath and that almost every utterance overlapped its neighbours, went something like this:

Beth: Isobel was in the kitchen and I was doing some gardening —

Hannah: While we waited to hear whether you'd found Jove —

Beth: And that blasted mutt Dover was trying to sneak in —

Daffy: So she had the catapult in her pocket. I was making up the pups' feed —

148

Hannah: While I was brushing them on the lawn here —

Beth: When that car pulled up at the gate and two men came in. One of them grabbed —

Hannah: Grabbed hold of me and asked —

Beth: In the most atrocious Glasgow accent —

Hannah: Demanded to know where Mr Cochrane was and when I said I didn't know he asked me where Mr Cochrane's dog was and when I said I didn't know that either he started to twist my arm. I can't think why he picked on me but —

Henry: Because you're the only one of the three of you who looks as though they might know something. Daffy looks like something from outer space and Beth looks younger than either of you. Now, will you please —

Beth: Anyway, Hannah started to struggle, she was yelping like a pup that's been trodden on —

Hannah: I was not!

Beth: And I could see that he was hurting her. I couldn't think what to do so I hit him with a slug.

Henry: Slug? What kind of a slug? Do you mean an airgun slug? You don't have an —

Beth: No, no, no. I had my slingshot handy only I'd used my last stone on Dover a minute earlier —

Hannah: And you know what a super shot she is when she's got her eye in —

Beth: Before I had time to think I'd loaded up with what was in my hand at the time and let fly —

Hannah: It was a simply huge slug, all soft and squishy, a monster —

Henry: You mean an invertebrate slug? A shell-less snail?

Hannah: Yes, yes, yes, of course. I had to duck my head out of the way or I'd have got it in the eye —

Daffy: And he opened his mouth to say something at that moment and I think it went right down his throat —

Beth: No, it couldn't have done, not all the way down, because he was coughing up bits of it for ages while he staggered round in circles with his eyes watering and the other one came at me and Daffy —

Daffy: And I'd just come out of the house with the puppies' feed so I hit him as hard as I could with the bucket, first in the middle and then over the head, and he fell down —

Beth: Not badly hurt —

Daffy: Not crippled for life unfortunately, but as well as being laid out for the moment he was covered in warm puppy mash and the pups were hungry —

Hannah: They're always hungry —

Daffy: And they jumped on him —

Beth: And they're six months old, they're not exactly little any more but still hyper-active —

Hannah: And they were jumping all over him and licking him and every time he opened his mouth to roar he got a tongue inside it and that seemed to scunner him more than anything else, I never heard such language in my life, I'm no prude but I was shocked, so I was going to hit him again with the bucket if I could have found a gap between the puppies —

Beth: But Isobel came out of the house and she'd seen all the fuss and flapdoodle going on so she brought your shotgun with her —

I had been letting the babble wash over me while I absorbed the general sense of it, filed away any portions which I might want to repeat, either to the police or for the amusement of my peers, and waited for the punch-line. But things were getting serious and it was high time that I took my part in the discussion. 'My Dickson?' I said. 'How would Isobel get her hands on that?'

'You went off in a hurry, remember?' Beth said. 'You took out the dart-gun and you left your gun safe unlocked.'

The police take the safekeeping condition on the Shotgun Certificate very seriously. I cast a frantic look around in case some lurking policeman was making notes. 'Don't ever say that aloud again,' I said. 'Don't even think it. Where is it now? She didn't put a dent in the barrels? Please tell me that she didn't let them take it away from her and go off with it!' Not only was the Dickson a very beautiful and valuable gun, but with the loss of Old Faithful it was the only gun to my name. If the police wanted to take such action they would have a legal battle on their hands to get the Dickson away from me, but it might have been within their power to prevent me from purchasing another gun — and the shotgun is an essential tool in the training of working spaniels.

'Relax,' Beth said. 'It's quite safe. And Isobel didn't have any ammunition for it. But they didn't know that,' she added soothingly. 'Isobel's standing guard over them now. With Old Irma. They were sort of disoriented because nothing like this had ever happened to them before, it must have been like being savaged by a pet gerbil, so they could easily believe that a sweet, middle-aged lady was quite pre-pared to shoot them.'

That much bore the stamp of credibility. 'Have you called the police?' I asked.

'Not yet.'

'We'll have to.'

'Yes, of course we will,' Beth said impatiently. 'The question is when. We thought you might want to ask them some questions first.'

I looked around. Reality was slipping away again. 'Where are they?'

'Where do you think? In the obvious place. We locked the two men in one of the quarantine runs, the one Jove was in. I took their wallets off them first.'

'And these,' Daffy said. She exhibited a cosh, a razor, two flick-knives and a knuckleduster.

I began to see a modicum of method in their madness, but it was not a method which should ever have been displayed to the press. 'Henry,' I said, 'would you and Mr Coutts please help Hannah to gather up the pups and kennel them again?'

'I'm coming with you,' Mike Coutts said. 'If you say that it's off the record then it's off the record until I have your permission to write it up. But if you think that I'm playing with puppies while you interview a couple of Glasgow heavies, you're dreaming.'

'Nothing was ever further off the record,' I said. Henry shot me a dirty look but he began to help Hannah to gather up the youngsters. They kept Sam with them.

I took the dart-gun from the car and led the way round the house. It was a wonder that I could walk at all, because I was simultaneously trying to look through the wallets and give Beth a précis of our discussion with Mike Coutts.

The area occupied by the quarantine kennels was enclosed on three sides by the old stone walls of what had once been a cattle court, cement rendered on the inside. The fourth side, originally open, was now fenced with welded wire mesh incorporating gates wide enough to admit a vehicle. Within this enclosure, which was now floored neatly in concrete, were the individual kennels and runs, separated from each other by low walls but once again topped and fronted with mesh so that the inmates could at least look out at the forbidden world as an antidote to the boredom of long confinement in quarantine. The dogs in residence were all at the wire, curious at the strange break in their routine.

Isobel stood at the outer gate, an incongruous figure in her pink-framed spectacles with my Dickson Round-action in her hands. 'Old Irma', sprawled on the paving outside the runs, looked the more formidable of the pair. Irma, an enormous and ancient German shepherd bitch, was the guard dog belonging to a vehicle repairer who, now that his busy season of icy roads was past, had taken his wife to the Canaries for a sunshine break. The son who always

154

guarded the premises during their absences brought his own guard dogs so that Irma, temporarily redundant, was deposited with us. She had been trained as a guard dog and knew exactly what was required of her. She looked and sounded the epitome of menace. In fact she was half blind, almost toothless and as amiable as a Labrador to her owners and their friends although she was much too lazy to fawn.

'We told them that Irma has rabies,' Beth whispered. 'I said that we're only waiting for the Veterinary Superintendent to come and certify it before destroying her.'

That, I admitted to myself, made sense. To anyone unfamiliar with the exact symptoms of rabies, Irma would be believable. A pair of gauntlets, a muzzle and other restraining gear at Isobel's feet suggested that the ladies had gone to some trouble to embellish the story with the sort of details that impart conviction.

The two men were also standing against the wire, although, unlike the other inmates, they were forced to stoop. It was not clear which of them had imitated the other, but a slight natural resemblance had been enhanced. They wore similar suits, once rather too sharp to be smart but now distinctly the worse for wear, and each had a slightly straggling moustache. They were below average height, thin-faced and, even seen at a disadvantage, they looked vicious. Looking at them through two layers of welded mesh and across ten yards of concrete, I thought that I would not have cared to have any member of my entourage meet them at closer quarters on a dark night. My look was met by twin glares from hooded eyes.

'You can't do this,' said the one whose suit was still damp and reeked of puppy mash. I could barely understand him. In general, the Glaswegian speaks good English, diluted by local slang (the Patter) and sometimes made almost incomprehensible by an accent which could crush gravel, unlike other broad Scots who speak a variety of dialects, all derived from the same Germanic tongue but which evolved in not very close parallel with the English language.

'We're doing it,' I said. 'Who sent you?'

I expected no answer and that's what I got, except that the first speaker called me a chanty-wrastler. The other man advised him to shut his geggie. Then the two fell stubbornly silent. But I had had some experience of dealing with 'dumb insolence' and in the light of the message 'Miss Johnson' had given us I could make an informed guess at the answer to my question. 'What did Nigel Heatherington hire you to do for him?' I asked.

If they worked for a gang leader they might well not know the name of the client, but I saw immediately that I had scored a bull. The two men looked anxiously at one another.

'Who?' said the speaker, much too late. 'You better leave us get now, Jimmy. We're not the right yins to mess with. We could come back and torch the place.'

'It's hopeless,' I said to Beth. 'These are hard men. They'll never talk. We'll just have to get rid of them.'

'We could let Old Irma bite them,' Daffy said helpfully. 'Then, when they're good and dead, they'd just be a couple of toughs who broke in looking for Mr Cochrane's dog.'

'Just a minute!' said the second speaker. 'Just a fookin' minute! You can't do that to another person. Rabies is a terrible way to die. The worst!'

'Shut up, you daft nyaff,' said the other fiercely in a hoarse voice. It was almost the first sound he had made other than a regular clearing of his throat followed by spitting. 'It's a bluff. Rabies can take all of six months to show. Any time up till then, we could get the shots.'

I brought into view the weapon I was carrying. 'Here's a better way,' I said. 'This is a dart-gun. I can put you both to sleep any time I like. How do you fancy waking up to find that you're out at sea in a leaking boat?'

Their expressions made it clear that they did not fancy it at all. For all the tough talk, I was becoming sure that their boss had only sent the Second or even Third Eleven to confront a household which, as far as he was concerned, was composed of females and a convalescent.

Beth's quick mind had spotted another lever to use. 'And how do you come to know so much about rabies?' she asked sharply. There was a furious silence. She turned her head to look at me. 'Cook and Simpson, Noel Cochrane's firm, they have something to do with rabies, don't they?'

Isobel, who had been practising mounting my Dickson to her shoulder and taking aim at the mid-sections of our captives, to their great discomfort, gave us her full attention. 'They have a hell of a lot to do with rabies,' she said. 'About three years ago, if I remember the guff in the veterinary journals correctly, they came out with a prophylactic treatment much cheaper than its predecessors. Instead of diploid cell vaccine cultured in human tissue culture they had gone back to the old rabbit brain tissue culture and got around the problems of severe reactions that had caused the method to be superseded — at least in this country.

'The cost of protective vaccination of domestic animals, and of wholesale broadcasting of treated bait to immunize

mammals in the wild, has been beyond the means of some of the poorer countries especially in the Third World, so no matter what the West, Europe in particular, did to push it back there was always more than one reservoir spreading it out again. But now, at least according to the Cook and Simpson publicity, a dramatic reduction in cost and therefore in both the incidence of rabies and the mortality rate was promised but I can't say that I've seen either reported so far. Of course, nobody ever reports good news . . .'

I looked at Mike Coutts. He shrugged.

'All the same, it begins to add up,' said Beth.

The two men had listened to this exchange with increasing perturbation. If some of the long words beat them, the general meaning did not. 'Listen, Missis,' said the first man. I was beginning to be able to tell them apart. This one had darker hair, an even narrower face than the other and the grooves that framed his thin moustache were more deeply cut. 'You'd better can it right there. You don't know what you're breengeing into.'

I could hear a faint tremor in Beth's voice which told me that she was taking the threats seriously, but she had too much courage to back down. As if he had not spoken she said, 'Let's see what we've got.

Cook and Simpson produced a new rabies medicine. Noel Cochrane spent at least a year in India as their representative. Selling the new product must have been a large part of his job. Then he came back to Britain when he was elevated to being promotions and marketing manager, or whatever they call the job. There were furious rows up to board level. Could it be that the new product wasn't as good as it's made out to be?'

I looked at Mike Coutts again, remembering that he had warned me not to put too much faith in rabies vaccines. He wore the trace of a smile.

'That could be it,' Isobel said. 'Mr Cochrane would have seen the product in use in India and would have been able to evaluate its performance. He may have seen that the product was less effective than its predecessor. I suspect that the changes made to prevent the sometimes serious reactions may have reduced its efficacy, and a slight reduction would be enough to allow the spread of rabies to continue. If he came home and found that the statistics had been massaged —'

'You're guessing,' said the second man desperately. 'The whole jingbang's just bloody guesswork.'

'So Noel had an attack of conscientious scruples,' Beth said. 'Very painful when it happens but it doesn't happen very often.'

There was a danger in assuming that Noel was among the angels. I decided to be devil's advocate. 'Or else he saw a chance for a little blackmail,' I suggested.

'That wouldn't be his line at all,' Daffy said. 'He's as straight as they come.' She saw us, even the men behind the wire, looking at her speculatively and she lifted her chin. 'Call it woman's intuition if you like,' she said defiantly.

'I call it sex,' I said firmly. All the same, I hoped that she was right. Daffy had a natural talent for reading men. I could have used her as an NCO. But in my experience the less charitable guess at somebody else's motives stood a good chance of being the correct one. 'Conscience or greed,' I said. 'He took away some papers proving that the firm had gone on the market with an imperfect product.'

'They wouldn't whip up a storm over bad publicity for the product,' Isobel objected. 'There'd be no point. If it was less effective than it was made out to be, that fact would inevitably emerge anyway, given a little time.'

'But,' I said, 'if there was proof that claims had been made which they knew at the time were unjustified, so that false confidence was generated and lives were put at risk —'

'Or even lost,' said Beth.

'— Or even lost, that could be much more serious. They could move heaven and earth to suppress that piece of intelligence. So they got a clue to Noel's whereabouts through his mobile phone and the boss's fixer was sent after him.'

'Jake Spurway,' Beth said, nodding. 'It was Jake, not Noel, who decided on a little blackmail.'

'Maybe,' I said. 'We only have that on the authority of somebody who wasn't exactly honest with us. Spurway may not be involved at all, or may be acting in his employer's best interests.'

'Possible,' Beth said. 'Either way, Harriet Williams, another of Noel's colleagues, was definitely involved and ahead of him. Either she was acting for Cook and Simpson or else she had blackmail in mind —'

'Or possibly a compromise between the two,' I said. 'Hope of a reward, in cash or promotion.'

'Could be,' Beth said. 'But she intended to step outside the law, or why would she steal a scooter to get here? Whatever, she headed here, knowing that Noel would want to collect Jove. She saw his case being loaded into my car so she pinched the car, complete with Jove. But somebody had had similar ideas and was watching her. He or they caught up with her at the lay-by and tried to take over, she resisted and she was killed — accidentally or on purpose.'

'They thought she was going to live,' Daffy said quickly. 'Otherwise they'd have put her in the car when they set fire to it.' Daffy looked at the two men beyond the wire mesh. 'You made a mistake there,' she said.

Both men started to protest but the original speaker won the floor. 'You can't stick us with that,' he yelped. 'You wee head-banger!' He continued in that vein for some time, but as his accent grew thicker with emotion I could soon understand no more than one word in three.

'Right,' said Beth when he had run down. 'Donald Aggleton was on the same track and got knocked on the head, non-fatally, while Miss Otterburn, the secretary of the big wheel, was trying to catch up with him to warn him about Jake Spurway's defection, or so she said.' She glanced at the two men, wondering whether to accuse them of the attack on young Aggleton but preferring not to provoke another outpouring of incomprehensible protest. 'These two charmers were sent to recover the documents and, in case they came back instead with the prospectus for a new worming powder, they were shown samples and told exactly what they were looking for.'

'That makes sense,' Isobel said. 'So what do we do with these two?' She looked as though she was quite prepared to take drastic action. I thought that she was bluffing but I was not sure. Nor were the two men. I could see that their neighbours, the dogs, smelled fear.

The darker one of the two began to say something but stopped abruptly.

'You don't need to do anything much,' said Michael Coutts. 'Do you know who I am?' he asked the men.

'How would we?'

'Then I'll tell you.' Mike laid it out for them — his identity, his newspaper connections and some of his earlier successes. 'Any nonsense from either of you,' he said, 'and I'll give them a very funny story about how you got captured by a girl with a guttie and you coughed up the whole story when she threatened to hit you in the eye with a slimy slug —'

'But that's not what happened,' the other man cried plaintively, as though that would be a conclusive argument.

'Maybe not,' Coutts said. 'But it's what the world and your boss will believe. The world will laugh until it busts a gut. Your boss won't be laughing.'

'In any case, we hand them over to the cops,' I told Beth and Isobel. 'Between us, we can witness that they came here, assaulted Hannah and threatened to burn the place down. But two can play at that game.' While Beth was fitting the known facts together I had had a second look through the two wallets. 'We have their addresses. MacClure, whichever one he is, has a woman — his wife, I hope — and two bairns in Pollockshields. The other one, Anderton, lives nearby. He has a photograph of an old lady, presumably his mother . . . Do you know what I was before I came here?' I asked the men.

'How could we?' the second man asked sullenly.

'He's killed more men than either of you,' Beth said stoutly.

'I never killed a soul,' squealed the more talkative man. 'Nor's he.'

'I was in the army.' I decided to embroider the truth. 'I served in the Falklands, in Northern Ireland and in the Gulf. And my wife's not wrong. I've killed more men than you've had hot dinners and I was an un-armed combat instructor for years. Now, you can come out and fight me, one at a time, and if you can get past me you can go. If not, we'll hand what's left over to the fuzz, explaining that you attacked me. And I'll pay a visit to Pollockshields afterwards. Now, which of you wants first go?'

I was bluffing. In my state of health I would not have been a match for either of them. I was banking on my underweight condition being taken for the leanness of perfect trim and on big city hard men being much less tough without their weapons.

The two men backed away from the wire. 'Loupin' Larry'll stiffen you for this,' said the more silent one.

'Hah!' Coutts exclaimed. 'That's what I've been waiting for. So Larry Gougan sent you. Just wait until he finds out — in print — that you two let his name slip. Guess who he'll stiffen then?'

Seven

Throughout our confrontation with the supposed hard men, Michael Coutts had lurked in the background, silent and more or less forgotten until the moment when he produced the threat which finally cowed the men into abject submission. When I came down off my second adrenalin high of the day and remembered his intent presence I half expected him to dash immediately to a phone. Mentally, I began to review the possible inducements which might postpone the more damaging of his revelations. But apparently he was unique among journalists. For one thing, his word was good. He seemed both amused and sympathetic. He drew me aside, but his only comment was a suggestion that we get the shotgun out of sight before the police arrived.

We left Isobel in charge again, without the shotgun but with the padlock still in place, Irma for moral support and Coutts as a witness, while we had a council of war in the kitchen, apprised Henry and Hannah of developments, slaked our dry mouths with tea and decided that our only possible course was a full disclosure to the police of everything except the brandishing of fire-arms. Those incidents, we agreed, had never happened. The Dickson vanished with the dart-gun into my gun safe.

In response to my phone call, a car full of uniformed constables arrived to take over the immediate responsibility from Isobel. It was followed hotly by Inspector Tirrell.

Old Irma had by then been withdrawn outside the compound and we skipped as lightly as we could over her part in the affair. We had had no business introducing her into the quarantine area in the first place, but the Inspector's mind was not thinking along the lines of the Animal Health Act 1981, or, it seemed, the Rabies (Importation of Dogs, Cats and Other Mammals) Order 1974 (as amended). The two captives, once they saw how fearlessly we handled the poor old bitch, never recognized their opportunity to make trouble for us.

Tirrell went through the motions of questioning us individually in the sitting room as a basis for formal statements to follow, but his manner was not censorious and it was clear that he was more amused than shocked by the incidents of the flying slug, the puppies' meal and the bluff with Irma. When he had extracted every scrap of information we had gleaned about the whole business — or at least those details we were prepared to disgorge — he called us together in the sitting room, Mike Coutts included, and spoke less formally.

'The facts seem to be clear,' Tirrell said. 'Your inferences are rather less so. What a pity that you saw fit to question the men yourselves!'

'Could you have got more out of them?' Beth demanded.

'Probably even less,' Tirrell admitted. 'But I'd have made sure that anything I did get out of them would be admissible in evidence.'

That was unfair. 'We've given you a little information,' I said indignantly. 'None of it except the admissions, for what little they were worth, came directly from those men, so whatever you can get out of them should be admissible. If you accept our inferences, your enquiries will be that much easier because you'll already know what you're trying to prove.'

The Inspector lost the last trace of his amusement and also of his pretence of being the dominating presence in full command. 'You think that you've made it easier?' he asked, and there was a querulous note in his voice. 'Dream on! You've cooked up a tenable theory on the basis of faint hints and uncertain clues. Slanting an investigation towards proving a particular theory is a road to disaster.' He sighed deeply and looked seriously put-upon. 'Because the suggestion has been made, somebody will have to go and question a very influential industrialist, who probably plays golf with the Scottish Secretary, and ask him whether he has been perpetrating what could well be regarded as a monumental fraud. Unfortunately, this is not the sort of enquiry that can be passed to the local force. Somebody will have to go through and conduct an interview personally and I don't see any of my superiors making a bid for that particular privilege. So I can make a good guess as to who that somebody is likely to be. And when Mr Heatherington denies it, as he will, and goes complaining to his important friends, I have nothing whatever solid to fall back on.'

There was an unhappy silence. Coutts broke it. 'If you have a damn bit of sense,' he said, 'you'll stay well away from Mr Heatherington and the rest of Cook and Simpson until you've done your homework properly. Start with the Department of Agriculture and Fisheries. If they don't have the statistics on rabies in Europe and the Third World they can certainly get them for you. So far, they've been cagey about letting me see them, but you should have more clout. If the real statistics contradict the figures put out by Cook and Simpson you've not only got your starting point; you'll find HMG and the Fraud Squad spearheading your enquiries.' Coutts paused. 'If you care to share such information as you can get —'

Inspector Tirrell still had some pride. He drew himself up. 'Leak it?'

'Whatever you want to call it. If you let me see the figures I may be able to help you interpret them. My researches will then be virtually finished. I'll be ready to make disclosures in the interval before the whole matter becomes *sub judice,* and my disclosures will certainly take the heat off you.'

The Inspector could hardly be expected to thank a journalist, but Tirrell went to his car looking a little happier. Before being driven away, he took a message over the radio and beckoned to me. 'They've identified those two men,' he said. 'Just riffraff. You'll have no more trouble from that quarter.'

It may have been because Mike Coutts was proving a man of his word or because he had turned out to be another dog-lover or just because he was a likeable person, but by then he was on friendly terms with Henry and myself, an honorary uncle to Sam and had become a favourite with the ladies of the firm. Henry and Isobel left to dine at home but at Beth's insistence Mike, as he had become, stayed to dinner and later accepted the offer of our spare room for the night.

I wondered, as I dozed before falling asleep, whether such quick acceptance might not be due to the practised charm of the professional journalist, but Mike made no moves towards our telephone or the one in his car and the morning papers reported sparsely on the continuing investigation into the death of Harriet Williams and mentioned the finding of an unconscious man near Lindhaven without connecting the two. No mention was made of any later developments.

I had fallen asleep late, but after the excitements of the day I slept deeply for once and Beth left me sleeping in the morning. When I came downstairs, washed and dressed but still half disoriented, Mike had helped the girls with the chores and then, while Beth attended to Sam, had taken over the duty of making breakfast. He did so with a more lavish hand than any of the usual cooks. As I worked my way through the unaccustomed bacon, egg, mushroom and tomato, I felt myself coming fully awake with at least a partial resurgence of my old energy.

Henry came with Isobel and then, when Isobel went off in his car to stock up with canine medicaments, he loitered in the hope of more dramas to break the monotony of retirement. Mike telephoned a contact in the police but learned only that Donald Aggleton, although now conscious, was suffering or feigning amnesia, that our two captives were maintaining a sullen silence and that there had been no sighting of Noel or of Jove.

We — Henry and Mike and I — were in the throes of debating whether there was any action that could usefully be taken when the phone rang. I had brought the cordless phone into the sitting room with me. I nearly left the call for Beth to answer in the kitchen; but I was half expecting a call from a shooting man whose wife had fallen desperately in love with one of our trained dogs but who had jibbed at the asking price. Beth might well have weakened in the face of her cajolery.

'Captain Cunningham?' said a woman's voice with a pleasantly neutral accent.

'Mister,' I said. 'Mr Cunningham. Speaking.'

'My name's Rodgers. Mrs Rodgers. I live in Ardunie.' (I pricked up my ears. Ardunie was less than five miles upstream from Lindhaven.) 'My nephew, Jim Phillips — he's the secretary of the Gundog Club —'

'I know him,' I said, but she rolled right on.

'— has only just told me that you're on the lookout for a lost Labrador. Is that right?'

'That's right,' I said. 'A large black Lab. A nice-looking beast. Male, no collar.'

'That sounds as if it could be the one. He's appeared at my back door the last couple of mornings, picking up the bread that I put out for the birds.'

The last thing I wanted was for a nervous old lady to call the police. 'He's very friendly,' I said. 'Quite harmless. He never ever bites. The worst he could give you would be a nasty lick.'

I heard a small chuckle. 'So I discovered. I gave him a meal of my leftovers and he wolfed it down. Of course,' she added, 'he may be visiting a dozen other houses as well.'

'Very probably,' I said. Labradors are entirely gut-oriented. A popular rule of thumb is that you can safely feed a puppy all that it will eat in ten minutes. That might be true of other breeds but in my experience ten seconds is enough for a Labrador pup while, on the other hand, I have had springers that needed to be coaxed and wheedled into eating at all. 'Does he seem all right?' I asked.

'He seems very fit. Nice shiny coat and a moist nose. And so friendly. I was hoping he was a stray that I could adopt.'

'Definitely not, if it's the right dog,' I said. It sounded as though there were no symptoms of rabies. 'He's the ewe lamb of a devoted owner. He was in a car when it was stolen. I'd better come and see you.'

'I'll be in all morning,' she said. I could hear the disappointment.

'If he's the right dog,' I said, 'there'll be a reward. And I'll help you to adopt another Lab from the dog's home.'

'Would you?' she said wistfully. 'I'd like that.'

Henry and Mike were ready to move. My half of the conversation and my evident excitement had been more than enough to alert them. 'Possible sighting of Jove at Ardunie,' I said. 'He seems to be making it a morning breakfast call and he's already made today's visit, but it's worth a poke around. Are you both coming?'

They were both coming. Beth, I think, was glad to see the back of us. Mike offered to take his car so that Beth and the girls would not feel stranded.

'Mine's already equipped for carrying a quarantined animal,' I pointed out. 'You couldn't even get the travelling box into yours.'

'Then I'll leave my keys on your hall table,' Mike said. 'They're welcome to the use of my car.'

Without the crate but with the travelling

box in the tail, we might not be legal for carrying a quarantined animal but at least we could use the back seats. If we found Jove, it would be a sign that our luck was running too high for any serious clashes with authority. Mike got in behind us. 'Where is Ardunie?' he asked as I settled myself in the driving seat.

'A village near the Tay,' I said absently. I was struggling with a recalcitrant key-ring, trying to remove the spare car key which jingled annoyingly while the car was in motion. 'In fact, it's not far from Lindhaven, where my old car was dumped, so it's hopeful.'

The two keys separated. I dropped the spare into the glove-box and we set off.

Despite the gloomiest prognostication of the forecasters it was a lovely morning, one of those spring mornings when you can be sure that winter will never come again, but I was in no mood to appreciate it. I wanted only to get on with the quest. Once Jove was recovered I would have fulfilled my responsibilities. From then on Noel Cochrane and all the others, police included, could work out their own damnations.

Mrs Rodgers lived in the last house of the village, a bungalow the back windows of which looked down a long slope of fields to woodland fronting the Tay. She was an elderly lady but still pretty and, like Henry, was delighted to have a break in the monotony of retirement. She took us into the back garden and showed us where she had fed her visitor. She showed us the bowl she had used, a souvenir of a Shetland collie which had died three winters previously. She invited us inside for coffee which was already prepared. I accepted for all of us. I wanted time to think.

Before we went inside, I tried a blast on the silent whistle. It set the local dogs barking but failed to conjure up a glossy black Labrador; and Jove's deep *bowff* was not to be heard among the others. So it seemed that he had not already been adopted by one of the neighbours.

The lounge was bright with floral wallpaper and a thousand ornaments and pictures. It had a broad window overlooking the fields, the woods and the Tay which, so far upstream, was down to a mere mile and a half wide. The hills in the distance rose out of a faint mist. They could have been cardboard cut-outs. The coffee was percolated and very good, and it was accompanied by small scones and pancakes and home-made raspberry jam. It was not long since my breakfast but, like the others, I found myself tucking in with appreciative little noises. Mrs Rodgers seemed pleased. I guessed that she had devoted her life to looking after her menfolk and now missed having someone to mother.

'I've asked around the neighbours,' she said. 'Your dog has called at most of the houses and been fed by at least half of them.'

'He'll be getting as fat as a pig,' I said sadly. 'Were all his calls made in the morning?'

'All of them. He seems to be a morning person.'

I decided to take a calculated risk. 'I think the best thing to do would be for us to come back first thing tomorrow,' I said.

She nodded brightly. 'I could put a collar on him if he comes before you're here.'

I nearly decided to invoke the police after all. This sweet old lady wanted to lay hands on an escapee from quarantine. Even if Jove proved clear, any hint that I had delayed in calling in the police, the local Divisional Veterinary Officer and the council would bring down the wrath of all three authorities on my head and those of my partners. But, judging from the happenings of the previous day, if an official search did happen upon Jove his chances of survival would be on a par with those of an airman whose parachute has failed to open . . .

'He might be nervous of a stranger trying to get hold of him,' I said, 'and then he probably wouldn't come back again. Don't worry. We'll be outside your back door from early morning. Ignore any sounds you hear. We'll let you know when we've got him.'

'If you're quite sure . . .' she said.

'I'm sure.' Mike was still working his way through the pancakes or I would have dragged us away. Mrs Rodgers had probably heard a whisper about a dog that had escaped from quarantine. Rather than give her time to connect the two incidents, I tried to change the subject. Miss Johnson's words came back to me. 'Are there any bothies around here?' I asked her. None of the crosses made on my map by my friend the water bailiff had been within ten miles of Ardunie.

'There used to be one or two, down by the river,' she said doubtfully. 'Just shacks that the anglers used for taking shelter. I think they've been cleared away now. Unless you mean Mr Spurway's place? He calls it "The Bothy" but it's more of a weekend cottage and a pretty luxurious one at that, so I'm told. You can almost see its roof from here.'

I must have goggled at her. During the worst of the long illness which had ended my days in the army, I had suffered occasional hallucinations. As the only available means of retaining a grasp on reality, I had developed the habit of weighing any very unusual occurrence before reacting to it. I was still wondering whether what I was hearing was real when Henry beat me to

179

the obvious question.

'By Mr Spurway, you mean Jake Spurway?'

'I believe that his first name's Jacob,' Mrs Rodgers said. From her tone I guessed that Jake Spurway was not a favourite with her.

'Of Cook and Simpson?' Henry persisted. He sounded as incredulous as I felt. It is not often that badly needed information bypasses all other seekers after truth and jumps up and down in front of us, making faces.

'I think so.'

'He has a weekend cottage here? For fishing? And he calls it "The Bothy"?'

'Yes, yes and yes.' Mrs Rodgers was beginning to sound impatient. 'Although I don't think that he's much of a fisherman. His brother used to come here for the fishing and stay for weeks at a time — that was before he was drowned, of course,' Mrs Rodgers said, in case there should be any misunderstanding on that point. 'He was a gentleman, Mr Paul Spurway. But not sensible enough to leave a will behind him. There was trouble in the family over the heads of it, I heard, and the upshot was that his brother Jacob took "The Bothy" for his share or part of his share of the estate. He comes through just as often as his brother ever did but he seldom comes alone.'

Here, clearly, was the root of her disapproval. 'Girls?' Henry asked in a shocked voice.

Mrs Rodgers nodded severely. 'Seldom the same girl twice. And the salmon isn't all that he's fishing for, I'll be bound,' she said.

Henry turned his face away to hide the gleam in his eye. 'I hope that's all that he catches,' he said solemnly.

Mrs Rodgers either missed or ignored the *double entendre*. 'Yes indeed,' she said.

The visiting Glaswegians had seemed to know nothing about any bothy, but their information had come from Mr Heatherington and it was believable, I decided, that the managing director of a large concern should know nothing of an employee's love-nest while at the same time his own secretary was well acquainted with it.

Mrs Rodgers pointed out a roof peeping through the treetops in the distance. We tore ourselves away from the delights of her coffee-table and returned to the car.

'Let's go and take a look,' Henry said.

I have never been one for precipitate action; impetuous infantry officers were a bad insurance risk and angels have been known to rush in where I fear to tread. The police would doubtless be pleased to learn that Jake Spurway had a weekend home in the vicinity. On the other hand, I wanted to have a very cautious look for Jove before letting loose another firing squad.

'Let's do that,' I said, 'but carefully.'

'Miss Whatshername said that there was nobody there,' Henry pointed out.

'There may have been nobody there at the time she visited,' I said. 'That's not to say that they're not there now.'

Following Mrs Rodgers' directions, we turned down towards the estuary through open farmland and made several turns onto ever more minor roads which soon reduced to a single, narrow lane with demarked passing places. It entered the trees which at that point bordered the estuary. A little further on we arrived at the mouth of what seemed to be a rough drive patched with gravel. There was no gate and no sign, but Mrs Rodgers' directions had been specific.

I reversed into the drive and drove back to the mouth of a track which I had noticed in passing. 'I'm going to park here,' I said. 'I don't know about you two, but I intend to approach very circumspectly on foot through the trees. There's some person or persons going around loose who've already knocked two people on the head, one of them fatally. Such things have been known to go in threes.'

'Discretion being the better part of valour,' Mike said, 'I'm sticking with you.'

'The police may have heard about this

place by now and picked him up,' said Henry. But he sat tight while I inched the car along the narrow track until it was hidden from the road.

'If the police had got him,' said Mike, 'I would have heard.'

I shooed Henry out and lifted the back seat.

'God's sake!' Henry said. 'You can't go visiting somebody's weekend cottage while bearing arms. You'll get every firearms certificate in the Region revoked.'

I showed him what I had taken out. 'Tranquillizer dart-gun,' I said. 'I have reason to believe that I may meet up with a dog which has escaped from quarantine. And both of you remember that I said it. Officially, we're looking for Jove.' All the same, I again filled the first dart with a load of tranquillizer that would have knocked out a St Bernard or an overweight politician. As an afterthought, I put Jove's rubber kangaroo in my pocket.

The others seemed content to follow my lead. The cart-track brought us out in a grassy field separated from the Tay by the broad belt of woodland. Ewes glared at us and gathered in the furthest corner, suspicious of our intentions towards their lambs, but we were hidden from the village by a swell of ground. For all I could see, the driveway might be close to that side of the woodland and I could make out the occasional glint of water between the trees, which suggested that we could easily be in full view of somebody screened by the shadows of the wood. Rather than expect Henry to move in a crouch I followed a line twenty yards out from the dry-stone wall, where a long dip helped to hide us.

Almost immediately, I began to glimpse the slated roof among the trees ahead. The dry stone wall enclosing the trees was topped with a single strand of rusty barbed wire but we came on a dilapidated narrow gate, provided for some purpose long forgotten. After a painstaking scrutiny of the trees, I untwisted the wires which had held the sagging gate closed and led the way through. The trees were deciduous and sparse, allowing patchy daylight to reach the ground, and any path that had ever been planned was now overgrown; but cattle or sheep had invaded the wood from time to time and made their own pathways. We followed in their tracks. Mike was cursing under his breath as mud and dung fouled his city shoes and brambles snatched at his suit. Henry was in his customary tweeds and stout boots and I had dressed, as usual, on the assumption that before the day was over I might have to crawl through the bushes after a lost dummy or a confused puppy.

The house stood in a clearing. Little attempt had been made at gardening, but the space was rocky and bright with assorted heathers and baby conifers. A hedge of yew had been planted around three sides of the clearing in the hope of providing a windbreak and although the plants had not exactly thrived in the thin soil there was some cover for our approach. The fourth side was open, with a tree-framed view to the Tay and the hills beyond.

The house itself was a mixture of ages. It seemed to have begun life as a rough, stone-built barn or cart-shed. This had been re-roofed, perhaps because of neglect, with a much tidier cladding of slates. Quite recently, windows and a door had been knocked out, with sills and lintels of concrete. The overall effect was eccentric but pleasing, even humorous, like that of a man trying to retain his dignity in a mixture of his gardening clothes and evening dress.

We came to a halt behind the thickest part of the hedge and studied the house. It sat there blandly, telling us nothing. There was no smoke visible at the only chimney, no milk on the doorstep, no paper in the letter-slot, no movement at the windows, no sound of music, no smell of cooking. The only sign of life was that a pair of swallows were nesting under the eaves. The house might have been empty for a year or be filled with muggers awaiting prey. There could even have been a comparatively innocent couple, sleeping late or enjoying each other's bodies. There was no way of telling. Anything was possible.

I checked that the ground was dry and seated myself, leaning back against a moderately comfortable rock.

'You're not going to take root there, are you?' Henry asked.

'Time spent in reconnaissance,' I retorted, 'is seldom wasted.' It had been a favourite dictum of my old general, the only wise words that I ever heard him utter.

'But there's nobody there.' We were out of the breeze in the wood. An insect buzzed around us and Henry waved angrily at it.

'Then why are you whispering? And do try to keep still,' I told him.

Henry dried up. He and Mike found seats and we kept watch through the threadbare twigs. Henry lit one of his rare cigars. Against the risk of the smoke being spotted from the house, it kept the midges at bay. Birdsong returned.

'There's no sign of a car,' Henry said peevishly.

'The way he — or she or it or they — has been operating,' said Mike, 'he'll be planning to steal another one as soon as he's finished whatever he's doing here. That's what he's saving up number-plates for.'

'If he's here,' said Henry. 'And if we're talking about the same person.'

'One of us could go and knock on the door,' Mike said.

'Are you volunteering?'

Mike shook his head.

I shifted myself and lay back, with the dart-gun across my chest and ready to hand. Crows were circling high above the treetops, much too cautious to settle while there were still men within gunshot. Their movement was hypnotic and I may have dozed off. I was roused by the alarm call of a blackbird. I could hear a car moving slowly along the drive, its engine jerking as the car lurched over the potholes.

'Don't move,' I whispered. In peripheral vision, movement draws attention when a motionless figure would remain unobserved. Henry and Mike, who had struck up a rapport, froze in the middle of a listless game of Paper Scissors Stone.

I sat up very slowly until I could peer out through the hedge. A Japanese hatchback with sporty lines was pulled up in front of the house and Miss Johnson (presumably alias for Kate Otterburn) got out. She stood for a moment, a stalwart amazon, straightening her skirt and patting her hair. She leaned back into the car for a moment, allowing us a glimpse of a pair of muscular thighs, and came up with a ladylike umbrella. I thought that she had more faith in the weather forecasts than in her own powers of observation. I was wrong.

The house door was suddenly open, framing a man. He was large, almost filling the doorway. His cannonball head was bald except for a fringe of dark hair worn short, but his face, despite a bold jaw and black eyebrows, was that of a man of no more than thirty. He was smartly but casually dressed in fawn slacks, a white shirt open at the neck and a sports jacket. His movements were fit and well sprung, the mirror image of hers. The overall impression that he gave was of toughness and self-reliance.

'You weren't followed?' he demanded.

'Not a chance!' she said gaily. 'The police questioned me for hours, my darling, and as far as they're concerned I'm as innocent as a babe unborn.'

His forceful face relaxed slightly.

'And you. How did you get on?'

He grinned suddenly, moved forward out of the shelter of his doorway and held up a small, plastic envelope. 'I've got it! A microfiche tucked under his toupee.'

'Really?' She sounded amused. 'I didn't even know that he wore a toupee.'

'Nor did I until the sticky tape in his case gave the game away.' The man laughed gruffly. 'It's a good one, must have cost him an arm and a leg.'

'You should ask him where he got it.'

'Nah,' the man said after a moment's thought. 'With me, what you see is what you get. He might have told me that much, but he wasn't going to say a word about the other thing, no matter what I did to him. And believe me, I did plenty. Come on inside.'

He turned back towards the door. She took quick steps across the weedy surface of the drive, coming up behind him. As she raised her ladylike umbrella, I thought that she was in playful mood. I expected a light patting sound and shouts of laughter. But the umbrella moved ponderously. The man must have seen her shadow move. He turned quickly so that the round-arm swing met his throat instead of the back of his neck. He went down with a thump, choking.

She stooped, snatched at the envelope and tucked it away. Without stopping to think, I took aim at her rounded behind and let fly. The tranquillizer dart took her in the left buttock. She straightened up quickly and stared round without seeing where the sting had come from. She passed a hand over her hip and dislodged the dart, looking at it without understanding. She took half a dozen paces back towards her car. But the dose that I had prepared had been in expectation of a large man. Just short of the car she went down on her face, out for the count.

There could be others. I had a charged dart in reserve. When I looked up from re-readying the dart-gun, Henry and Mike were already standing between the two prone forms.

Henry produced his mobile phone. 'Police?'

'And ambulance,' Mike said urgently as I arrived beside them. 'Ambulance first. This man's choking to death.'

Henry looked hard at the fallen man and pushed his phone into Mike's hand. 'You make the calls. Unless you've ever opened up somebody's windpipe?'

'Never. But have you?'

'No. But I went on a first-aid course once and we were shown how to do it.' He turned to me. 'Have you got your little lock-knife on you?'

I was about to ask whether Henry should be embarking on a surgical career at his age, but the man on the ground, who I presumed to be Jake Spurway, had turned the colour of a stormy sky near sunset and was making strange noises. He would be dead long before we finished arguing. I produced my knife. As far as I could remember it had been washed since I had last used it to paunch a rabbit, but there was no time to worry about that.

Mike's voice was engaged on the phone in a patient explanation of how to find the place.

As I watched anxiously, Henry felt for the Adam's apple and then measured with his fingers a small distance below it. He hesitated. 'If all goes well,' he said, 'I'll get a medal; otherwise, I'll be a reckless jackass who ought to be locked up, if not something worse. Decision time.'

'Tracheotomy time,' I said. 'You have to do it.' Henry sighed and moved the knife and I looked away.

Suddenly the choking stopped and there came the sound of somebody snatching breath, the sound distorted by slurps and wheezes. 'Sod it!' Henry said. 'It keeps trying to close up. Have you got any kind of a tube that I can use? In the stories they use a pipe-stem although that would be on the small side.'

None of us smoked a pipe. I felt in my pockets. 'Will this do?' I asked.

'For the moment. It's still too small. See if you can find something bigger. More like the size of a pencil. The shell of a Biro might do. Try the house.'

Mike seemed to have finished his phone calls. 'Come and help me look,' I said.

I held the dart-gun at the ready as we entered. The accommodation was all in a single large room except that the door stood open on an obviously empty shower and toilet compartment. Kitchen units and a cooker stood against one wall. A corner held several bunks and a double bed, which seemed to have been an afterthought. There was an area devoted to comfortable chairs around a huge fireplace.

Noel's attaché case or one very like it was open on a low table but there was nobody, living or dead, to be seen. Noel, I thought sadly, was unlikely to have been released alive, whatever the motivation of the man outside. Perhaps Noel had been buried in some nearby field or his weighted body dropped in the Tay. Meanwhile, my immediate concern had to be with the more or less living, if only to see that he stood trial for his sins.

I began a hasty search of the drawers and cupboards.

'Quiet a moment,' Mike said. 'Listen!'

I listened but my hearing was dulled by years of shooting and I could only hear the blood in my ears. Mike homed in on a large oak chest and wrestled with the key. I noticed that a row of small holes had been punched through it and fragments of wood and sawdust littered the floor.

The lid came up. A man's figure was crammed inside. He seemed unconscious but, to my relief, I could see that he was breathing. The square face looked battered like that of a boxer after losing a major fight and the head was unexpectedly bald, but beneath the blood smears I recognized Noel Cochrane.

Eight

Now with three unconscious bodies to worry about, I was beginning to wonder where it would end and how I should apportion my help. I was more friendly disposed to Noel but, although damaged, Noel was breathing of his own accord while the man outside needed all the help he could get and possibly more. The woman, on the other hand, was my personal victim and I was none too sure whether the dosage that I had given her, which had been prepared with the memory of Hector Tholess in mind, might not have been an overdose.

Mike had lifted Noel into a sitting position. The contents of Noel's pockets had spilled into the bottom of the chest along with the displaced toupee. I saw a slim, gold ballpoint pen which seemed to be about the size I was looking for. I snatched it up. The metal was slippery, the mechanism unfamiliar, and nothing I could do would take it apart. Henry might be able to figure it out.

'I'll be back, maybe,' I told Mike. 'Do what

you can for Noel until the ambulance comes.'

I carried the dart-gun outside again. And there I saw what I had been looking for all the time. The dart lay where it had fallen in the dust. It might be unhygienic but it was the right size. I recovered my knife from Henry and with its help I took the syringe apart and wiped the barrel out with an almost clean handkerchief.

The woman must have had the constitution of an elephant, or else I had spent longer than I thought inside the Bothy because she was already stirring. I removed the ignition key and locked up her car. There was a handbag on the back seat and, presumably, if she had a spare key it would be in that.

The scene had changed in another way. The tracheotomy patient breathing heavily and regularly through my silent whistle must have been sending signals far and wide. A long-haired mongrel was sitting, awaiting events, and I saw a collie come out from among the trees.

Henry was crouched uncomfortably over the man whose eyelids, I saw, were flickering. I squatted beside Henry and gave him the tube. 'About bloody time,' he said.

'He was lucky that you were shown how to do it.'

'We were also told never to attempt it,'

Henry said. 'But how do you stand by and let someone die?'

'You don't,' I said. I pushed aside a bearded collie which had made an appearance and was investigating the blood. 'Not even somebody who had been knocking hell out of Noel Cochrane. He's inside, battered but still alive.'

'That's who it was? I wondered.'

I could hear an ambulance approaching and, further off, a police car.

Henry, still squatting down, almost threw my silent whistle at me. His fingers were bloody and he had been further sprayed by his patient's first breaths. My whistle was so stained with blood that I almost refused to pick it up. But it had done its job. With the new tube in place, Jake Spurway was breathing deeply and easily. Somebody would have to shoot him full of antibiotics and clean up the incision from Henry's rudimentary tracheotomy, but we had done the best we could. And although the whistling had stopped, dogs were still arriving. I could see a German shepherd coming through the trees.

There was a sudden snuffling in my ear. I turned my head and found myself eyeball to eyeball with a black Labrador. Before I could move, he dropped the rubber doll which he had been carrying and gave my face a thorough lick. The Labrador was

Jove. He was grinning idiotically, so pleased to be back with friends that his whole rear half was waggling, but not forgetting to pick up the rubber doll which he had abstracted from somebody's garden. I offered him his red kangaroo and after a moment he spat out the rubber doll and grabbed for it with a grunt of delight.

It was a moment of heady relief. I am easily moved to sympathy for dogs, far more so than for humans, because dogs do not understand. There is no way to explain that you will return, that the vet will make it all better, that they cannot come shooting to-day because that is not what today is about. They cannot work out that their misery is finite and will some time end, and so their misery is magnified.

'If somebody would find me some sticking plaster or masking tape or even Scotch tape,' Henry said plaintively, 'maybe a piece of string or I could get by with some Blu Tac, I could then fix this tube and allow myself the luxury of finding out whether I can still stand up. I'm too old for Cossack dancing.'

Jove pushed me over and tried to lean on me but I shoved him away and got up. 'No time,' I said. 'Mike's resuscitating Noel Cochrane and I must put Jove in the car before the police get here. That way, it's as though he'd never been AWOL. Just grit your teeth and hold on.'

'You're sure Noel's all right?'

'How all right is all right? He's been knocked around and cooped up in a wooden chest. But he's alive and likely to remain that way.'

'Good. And you're sure that's Jove?'

In my relief I was ready to laugh at last. 'Positive,' I said.

'And you're sure he doesn't have rabies?'

My amusement deserted me. I had forgotten that possibility. 'As positive as one can be,' I said.

'Then you can sit here and hold the tube in place while I take Jove back to the car.'

'I don't have a lead here,' I said. 'Are you certain that Jove would follow you? You've hardly met.'

'Go then,' Henry groaned. 'Bring me back a physiotherapist and a chiropractor to straighten me out again between them. They can take a leg each.'

I started to put the dart-gun down beside Henry but he waved it away. 'No need for that,' he said. 'If he turns stroppy, all I have to do is pull the tube out.'

I picked up the umbrella which was lying nearby. Although it was now looking distinctly secondhand, I could see that it had been dismantled and reassembled very neatly around a length of lead pipe. I dropped it beside him. 'And the young lady?' I asked. 'Suppose she comes at you, foaming at the mouth?'

He glanced at Miss Otterburn, who was sitting up and shaking her head. She did not seem to be at peace with the world. Henry put out his spare hand for the dart-gun. 'You have a point,' he said.

I called Jove to heel and set off back through the trees by the way that we had come. As I loaded him into the travelling box I heard the ambulance go by. A car passed in the opposite direction while the klaxon of the approaching police car was still some way off. If I confronted the police with Jove in my car, I would be in contravention of the regulations and somebody might still make trouble. I reminded myself to press the security switch, started the engine and set off for home in a hurry. The new car sighed as though realizing that the honeymoon was over before it had begun.

There was an irreducible minimum of time that had to be spent telling Beth and the girls the bare bones of what had happened and handing out instructions for the care and incarceration of Jove and the notification of almost everybody in the world who had the least vestige of authority, but I managed to be on my way back within about twenty minutes. Even so, by the time I was nearing the Bothy I guessed that the driveway would be jammed with official vehicles.

I left my car in the track where it had been earlier and walked.

The scene had changed again, this time radically. The wounded had been removed by ambulance. Henry had risen or been lifted to his feet on which he was now hobbling pitifully around the gravel. What seemed at first glance to be a whole battalion of police officers turned out on closer examination to be less than a dozen, of whom those who were not following Henry around and asking him questions were milling around in apparent aimlessness which on closer examination turned out to be a painstaking search of the landscape for something unspecified. A man with a medical bag was getting into one of the cars.

Our old friend Inspector Tirrell seemed to be in charge. He headed across the gravel to intercept me but I dodged him and shot a hasty glance inside the building and came back. One face was definitely missing. 'Where's Mike?' I asked Henry.

'God knows,' Henry retorted unhappily. 'He helped to bring Noel out to the ambulance and then shot off on foot before the police got here, leaving me to try and explain events which I only partially understand. My suspicion is that he's gone to find a phone and sell the story.' He looked at me shrewdly. 'Was all well at home?'

'Fine,' I said. 'How are the patients?'

Henry stretched and I heard a joint crack. 'If you include me, I am in desperate need of a hot bath, strong drink, a massage, traction and some tender loving care, thank you for asking.'

'I meant the others,' I said.

'Oh. Mostly they were in better shape than myself, having comparative youth on their side. The man — who may or may not have been Jake Spurway — was breathing. They had a proper tracheotomy tube for him. Noel was still woozy and he seems to have a couple of broken ribs to go with sundry sprains.'

I noticed for the first time that the Japanese hatchback had vanished. 'And the girl?' I asked.

'Drove off. She had a spare key for her car in a magnetic box under the back wing.'

'You let her go?'

'What would you have had me do?' Henry asked in exasperation. He gave me a meaningful look. 'You left the dart-gun with me for purposes of self defence. Didn't you?'

'Of course,' I said, belatedly catching on.

'Well, then. I couldn't leave my patient to die. I did threaten to ping her up the backside with your dart but that wouldn't have been self defence and anyway she told me to get knotted,' Henry said indignantly. 'I don't know what women are coming to! She was in her car with the door closed before I could bring myself to do it. It's against my religion to shoot girls in the bum,' he added, with an air of conscious virtue.

Inspector Tirrell had been waiting patiently, no doubt hoping that we would let slip some incriminating morsel. Abandoning any such hope he broke in on us. 'If you've quite finished telling each other all about it, perhaps it's my turn to be informed. Please come inside.'

When my eyes adjusted from the strong sunlight outside I saw that the interior of the Bothy was, if anything, rather tidier than before. The two constables who were still engaged in a search must have been inexperienced in the ways of the CID. They were meticulously replacing everything in an orderly manner, which was not in accord with my earlier experience of police searches. The fact that they were WPCs may have accounted for the unusual consideration. The oak chest had already been removed.

The stuffed leather armchairs were old and worn but had settled over the years into comfortable shapes. I thought that they had probably come from some hotel or club. Henry and I settled into two of them while Tirrell stood with his back to a large stone fireplace holding long-dead ashes. He looked displeased. It seemed that the days of informal chatting were over.

'Mr Cunningham,' the Inspector began sternly, 'you left the scene of a crime.'

'I left two perfectly good witnesses here,' I said, choosing my words carefully. 'It wasn't my fault if one of them went off. On the other hand, I had recovered the dog which had escaped or been stolen from quarantine. I returned it to secure accommodation, which I was legally obliged to do, and came straight back here. What would you have preferred me to do?'

'I will ask the questions,' the Inspector said coldly.

'I think you'll find,' I said, 'that I have the right to ask questions too.'

Without commenting, the Inspector made a note. My arguments were sound as far as they went but he looked no less peevish. It is always annoying to be robbed of a good grievance. 'Leaving that for the moment,' he said, 'Mr Kitts has given me an outline of the story but he admits that his knowledge may be incomplete. We'll get down to a formal statement later. For the moment, please tell me everything. Everything,' he repeated.

It was a tall order but I tried to comply with it. I told the Inspector everything of even marginal relevance I could call to mind that had happened since the previous evening.

'You didn't think to keep me advised of your activities,' he said. He sounded more angry than hurt.

'What activities?' Henry demanded. 'We had a report of a Labrador on the loose so we came to take a look. Miss Otterburn had paid us a call several days ago, we think in the hope of picking up information or triggering some revealing actions —'

'Or to pass a message warning the young man Donald off,' I said.

'Or that,' Henry said testily. 'Where was I? Yes. During that visit she let slip something about a bothy. Our informant told us that this place was known as "The Bothy". In view of the possible connection, it seemed that the dog might have fetched up near here, so we came to take a look. While we were looking, we saw the lady arrive and whack the occupant, who we believe to be Spurway, over the head. We called you immediately. At what earlier point do you think we should have called you in?'

'What's more,' I said, 'the only efforts I was making were directed towards recovering the dog. Alive,' I added. 'I was not going to issue you with an invitation to bring along another firing-squad. You saw the mood that Tholess was in.'

His nostrils flared slightly but he decided against joining battle. 'The man had identification on him,' he said, 'including a work pass with his photograph. There can be no doubt that he was Jake Spurway and that he was employed by Cook and Simpson. If, as you suggest, the woman was Miss Otterburn, secretary to the managing director, then they were colleagues.'

'That would seem to follow,' said Henry.

'Colleagues,' Tirrell repeated. 'But they can hardly both have been working in the firm's best interests.'

'Unless they were in competition with each other in the hope of a reward or promotion,' Henry said.

The Inspector took a few moments for thought, frowning, and decided to shy away from speculation. 'We haven't found any envelope. You say that the young woman took it?'

Henry nodded. 'The last that I saw of it, she was tucking it into her underwear.'

'I wonder,' the Inspector said absently. 'You've spoken with her so you're entitled to an opinion. Would she have been one to act on her employer's behalf? Or on her own? Or even for some other party altogether? Would she have been capable of taking single-handed initiative or was she being led by somebody else? You're sure that you didn't overhear anything else, something that might give me a clue to her real motivation? What do you think?'

He was only thinking aloud. I decided that

he had a blasted nerve, seeking our opinions after ticking me off, but there was no point saying so. 'Nothing,' I said.

Henry was less inclined to pass up the chance of pontificating to a policeman. 'Starting from the beginning,' he said, 'it seems that Noel Cochrane came away from his work with some valuable information. It may have had to do with a forthcoming takeover or a new cure for the mange, that doesn't matter. Jake Spurway, the MD's fixer, came after it. He is said — by an unreliable authority — to have wanted it on his own behalf. Spurway may have been acting in his employer's interests and Miss Otterburn may have tried to cut a piece of the action, on her own behalf or with a partner.'

The Inspector seemed ready at first to bite Henry's head off, or at least to invite him to give his long-deceased grandmother a lesson in egg-sucking, but Henry's words seemed to have started a train of thought. 'But he has to be the prime suspect for the murder of Harriet Williams and clearly he kidnapped and interrogated Mr Noel Cochrane,' he pointed out.

'He may have done so on his employer's behalf,' Henry pointed out. 'Excessive force but well intentioned. He may not have meant Miss Williams to succumb. We've been assuming that Spurway was the villain, but that was because Miss Otterburn told us that Spurway had turned his coat. And, of course, one tends to think of coshing as a male form of violence; but when we saw Miss Otterburn swing that umbrella, I was reminded that behind every violent man there's a woman screaming, "Kill the bastard!" Has Donald Aggleton recovered enough to say who hit him?'

The Inspector decided to open up. 'Mr Aggleton recovered consciousness this morning. His memory is patchy but he thinks that he was hit from behind and never saw his attacker. He is adamant that he was acting alone and trying to recover some material, the nature of which he refuses to discuss, on behalf of his employers.'

'He'd be bound to say that,' I pointed out.

'Of course.' Tirrell dismissed the thought as not having been worthy of mention. 'He says that he knew about this place and was heading in this direction when he saw Spurway driving by in what must have been your car, the old one. He decided to spy on him. After that, his memory seems to be genuinely patchy.'

'Then where is his car?' I asked.

'We found it in a car park in Cupar,' said Tirrell.

'Miss Otterburn,' Henry said, 'seems to have been making up to Jake Spurway and yet we saw her lay him out with a lead pipe hidden in her brolly. You shouldn't close your mind to the possibility that she was the evil genius from the beginning.'

'I'm not,' said Tirrell patiently, 'any more than I'm closing my mind to the fact that I have only your words for these critical pieces of evidence. We have found no trace of the envelope, containing something apparently of great value, which you tell us you heard Spurway claim to recover from Cochrane and you saw Miss Otterburn remove from Spurway's unconscious body.'

Henry and I exchanged glances in which surprise was mixed with a trace of excitement. It is not every day that one gets suspected of involvement in high-level chicanery.

'Well, you can search me,' Henry said at last.

'I intend to have both of you searched,' said the Inspector. 'Not that it will do me much good. Mr Cunningham had ample time to dispose of a hundred microfiches — if that is really what this is all about.'

'And again you have only our word for what was said,' Henry acknowledged. 'Tell your minions to do their damnedest, Inspector. I only ask that you tell the young ladies to warm their hands.'

'You should be so lucky!' I said.

I heard one of the WPCs suppress a faint

snort of amusement but Inspector Tirrell flushed. He sent them outside and called in a male constable to perform the search.

Half an hour later, after being searched apologetically by the young constable — with warm hands — we were back in our two chairs and Inspector Tirrell had resumed his dominant position in front of the dead fire.

'Since you were rash enough to leave the scene,' he said to me, 'you realize that your house will have to be searched.'

'You have a warrant, or whatever they call it?' Henry asked.

'I could get one, although strictly speaking I wouldn't need it. Are you going to be awkward?' The Inspector was still looking at me.

'Probably not,' I said. 'But you do realize that that damned woman almost certainly ran off with the microfiche, if that's what it was? And, even if she didn't, that searching my house would surely be a waste of time, because I could have left the envelope with a friend, put it in the post to myself or hidden it anywhere along my route?'

'I do. But I'm under orders.'

I can be as awkward as the next man on my day, probably more so, but this did not seem to be the time for more than a token objection. 'Personally,' I said, 'I don't give a damn provided that I get a written undertaking that you'll reinstate any damage and leave the place more or less as you found it. But my wife may have something to say. We were searched once before, unnecessarily and unproductively, and she regarded it rather as an indecent assault. If she says it's all right, go ahead. If not, try to get a sheriff to sign a warrant and I'll have a dozen lawyers tripping you up.'

Wisely, Tirrell decided to ignore any question of remedial work. 'Call her up and put it to her, then.'

'Oh no,' I said. 'You want permission to search without a warrant, you ask her yourself. She'll probably set Irma on you. I'm going home now. You may come with me if you insist.'

'Stay where you are.'

He came to stand over me. The Inspector's words and tone were firm enough but I could see that he was uncomfortable. The perfect moment for being bloody-minded might not yet have arrived, but it would have to do. 'I am hungry,' I said. 'I am also a busy man. We've been nothing but cooperative. You have already searched us. Either arrest me or get the hell out of the way.' I began to get up, forcing him to step back.

There was a sudden change of tone. 'Please wait. One minute.' Tirrell stepped between the chairs and left the building, leaving us alone together for the first time since my return. Through the open doorway I could see him speaking on a personal radio.

'Here's a turnaround!' Henry said comfortably. 'The Inspector is, as he says, under orders and he doesn't like them one damn bit. On what he's got, I don't think any sheriff would issue a search warrant and if he goes ahead without one and is wrong you can raise a stink. He forgot my portable phone. Do you want to call your solicitor?'

'I won't bother. There's nothing in the house I'm ashamed of. Warn Beth, if you like. As far as I'm concerned, home is a roof for keeping the rain off whatever I happen to be doing at the time, but she thinks of it as an extension of herself.'

'All right,' Henry said, producing his phone. 'Beth will undoubtedly chew the Inspector's balls off.' He sounded rather pleased at the prospect.

The Inspector returned a few minutes later. 'There's been a delay,' he said. 'You can go home now — accompanied, of course.'

'A delay to who or what?' Henry asked sharply.

'There are people coming,' Tirrell said. He turned away before we could ask any more awkward questions.

In the event, we were kept waiting for some little time while the Inspector wound up his operations at the Bothy. Realization seemed to dawn simultaneously on all of us that we had been on our feet for a long time. Rather than walk to my car, Henry and I and the two male constables packed into Tirrell's Range Rover and were driven round to the mouth of the track where I had left my car.

That was where we hit a snag. The car had vanished.

The sense of *déjà vu* roused me to fury. This was not my clapped-out old banger but my newest toy, apple of my eye, and it might well have vanished while I was being unnecessarily delayed by the Inspector. I drew breath, preparing to blow my top.

Henry forestalled me. 'Don't waste time, John. Whoever took it is probably half a mile up the road, trying to restart it. Get back in the Range Rover.'

Tirrell did not waste time asking questions. He directed his driver towards the main road and just short of it we came on my abandoned car. When the engine died on him the driver had managed to freewheel into a track which slanted downhill at an easy angle, but the car was still in full view of the road. The Range Rover pulled in to the side and we walked down. One window had been broken but otherwise it was un-damaged.

The sense of relief that flooded through me did not extend to allowing Tirrell to impound the car for forensic examination. As I pointed out, rather forcefully, I had great need of the car and its contents, whereas what he was likely to learn from an examination by his technicians could equally be discovered by means of a quick inspection and the taking of samples out-side my front door. Whether proof that some individual had at some time driven my car could be of any possible use to him was something which, I said, I would leave unexplored.

Tirrell seemed ready to argue from a po-sition of strength. I resolved the matter by getting into the car, in my indignation al-most falling over a tine harrow which the local farmer had left inverted nearby while he replaced some of the spikes. I pressed the secret switch and ground the starter. After a few seconds, during which time Tirrell was ordering me to cease and desist, the engine fired and I drove off. Half a minute later the Range Rover was large in my mirror. I was relieved to see that Henry was aboard it; Inspector Tirrell would have been quite angry enough to leave him stranded. There was another police car fol-lowing the Range Rover.

The cavalcade turned in at the Three Oaks gates at last and I pulled up behind Mike Coutts's car, which was still sitting where he had parked it the previous evening. Tirrell came out of the Range Rover like a clay pigeon out of a trap but, before he could vent his spleen on me, Beth came out of the house with the cordless phone and pushed it into Tirrell's hands. 'For you, Inspector.' Then she rounded on me. 'You've missed lunch again. You know damn well you're supposed to be on a regular regime. There's a snack on the kitchen table. For Henry too.'

'Thanks,' I said humbly.

The mixed grill on the kitchen table was still piping hot and rather more than a snack. The long morning of activity had given us both an appetite. Inspector Tirrell arrived in the kitchen doorway and looked with distaste at us gorging ourselves. I was sure that I heard a faint rumble from his stomach.

It seemed only polite to say something. The Inspector, after all, was a sort of guest in my house. 'Starting your search, Inspector?' I asked vaguely.

'That was the Procurator Fiscal on the phone,' he told me. 'Your solicitor is already with a sheriff in chambers, asking for an interdict to prevent me from applying for a search warrant unless he is present to

214

oppose it. The words "frivolous" and "vexatious" were bandied about. The Procurator Fiscal pointed out that the sheriff has no power to make any such order, but it was an effective delaying tactic as well as a way of rubbing my nose in the fact that you knew I was coming. And a fat chance I'd have of getting a warrant,' he added bitterly, 'when both Miss Otterburn and that damned journalist had left the scene. What I'd like to know is how your solicitor came to know so much detail about the case.'

Beth who, during this harangue, had been on the phone to Hugh Morris about a replacement window for the car, left the room quietly and I heard her getting Sam up after his nap.

'I did not phone him,' I said. 'As I told you, I didn't give a damn if you searched the place. I still don't.'

'Well, it's going to look bad.'

'To whom?' Henry asked.

'Anybody. Everybody.'

Tirrell, clearly, was under pressure. He went out onto the gravel and sent away most of his search team. He returned accompanied by one sergeant. Beth came back with Sam. Remembering that the police had been on the go for at least as long as Henry and myself, she offered them food. They refused a cooked meal, but apparently it was permissible to accept a chair and a sandwich, even from members of the public who were being obstructive at the time.

Henry looked round from his seat at the scrubbed table that filled the middle of the large kitchen. The two policemen, in a vain attempt at effacement, had taken the two basket-chairs by the Raeburn which were, perhaps coincidentally, the most comfortable in the room if not the house.

'What are we waiting for now?' Henry asked.

Inspector Tirrell hastily swallowed a large mouthful of egg and cheese sandwich. 'If I knew that,' he said, 'I still couldn't tell you.'

Sam chose that moment to go off into peals of laughter. Children can be remarkably adept at reading the emotions of their elders.

'Oh, them!' said Henry.

As the afternoon wore on without any sign of a second wave of visitors, Inspector Tirrell settled himself on the seat below the kitchen window, prettily framed by a clematis in full blossom, and kept an eye on the scene, occasionally exchanging a few words with some distant colleague by way of his radio. It was turning into a beautiful evening of soft light and the music of birds but the Inspector did not seem to be getting any pleasure out of it. From time to time a dog on exercise would detour to sniff his ankle and would receive a look which dared it to proceed further.

His sergeant, however, Cox by name, showed an intelligent interest in the running of the kennels and even lent a hand by carrying dogfood for the girls, firing blank cartridges and later throwing dummies on the lawn while I instilled steadiness into young spaniels who wanted nothing more than to hurl themselves impetuously into the game. Later still, he played with Sam on the sitting-room floor until the exhausted child was ready for bed.

The daylight faded, the day's work was as nearly finished as it ever is and a meal was dished up — later than usual in view of the lateness of Henry's lunch and mine. Henry and Isobel had stayed to eat with us, as was their habit in times of stress. We were interrupted when the sound of tyres on the gravel warned of the arrival of an otherwise silent car.

By then the two policemen had withdrawn to the sitting room, Inspector Tirrell again making do with a sandwich and a cup of coffee. Sergeant Cox was also provided with a sandwich but, unknown to his superior, Beth had repaid him for his assistance by feeding him a hot meal, course by course, as it came off the stove. The Sergeant was still young enough to have an appetite. We heard his footsteps go to the front door and return, accompanied. The sitting-room door closed again but we could hear, faintly, the murmur of voices.

'The Inspector,' Henry said, 'will be enjoying the pleasure of explaining why the promised search has not been carried out.'

That reminded me. 'You never said why you got the lawyers to kick up such a fuss about the Inspector looking the place over,' I reminded Beth.

She looked at me without expression. 'You think I should have welcomed them? We still haven't got quite straight after the first time and that was — what? — about five years ago.'

'On the other hand,' I said, 'on that occasion they did turn up several things I thought had been lost for ever. I think you're up to something.'

'Did you know that there's a bobby in uniform outside the gates?' Hannah asked. 'And another lurking at the back?'

That broke my train of thought. 'I didn't,' I said, 'but I can't say that I'm surprised. Nothing would surprise me any more.'

'The village will be wondering what we've been up to,' Isobel said.

'They'll have made up their minds,' Hannah said. 'You wouldn't believe the stories that'll be going around by now.'

'Don't worry about it,' said Beth. 'Tomorrow we'll spread a rumour that we asked for police protection because there was so much money in the house.'

'Before you get us burgled,' I said, 'you'd better check up on our insurance. And the shopkeepers will double the price of everything.'

Ten minutes later, when we had finished eating, Inspector Tirrell appeared in the kitchen door with Sergeant Cox at his shoulder and beckoned to me.

But we in the kitchen had resumed a technical discussion of far more immediate importance. From time to time one gets a spaniel pup which is unduly finicky about its food and needs to be coaxed or jump-started into eating; but when three young dogs which had formerly been greedy feeders simultaneously go off their victuals just at a time when there is a noticeable change in the appearance and texture of the basic feed, it is time for some fresh thinking. Beth, a realist, took the view that the dogs would soon start eating again when they got hungry. Hannah wanted to return to our previous brand even if it could not claim to be as rich in calcium and vitamins. Daffy had been overcoming resistance with the aid of blends of added flavourings and wanted to continue along those lines while Isobel, ever the scientist, wanted to turn the whole thing into a research project.

The Inspector was ignored, except that I

favoured him with a quick shake of the head.

'The Inspector,' Sergeant Cox said, politely but firmly, 'is inviting Mr Cunningham to come to your sitting room.'

'And Mr Cunningham,' Daffy retorted, 'is telling him to sod off. Rabbit gravy,' she added to the Inspector's evident puzzlement.

'Carry on as you're going,' I said to Daffy. 'We'll see how they take to the next batch. I wasn't going to be so rude as that,' I told the Inspector. 'Nearly, but not quite. I don't mind coming to the sitting room; it is, after all, my own room as the Sergeant's well-chosen words reminded us. But Mr Kitts comes with me.'

'We'd prefer to see you on your own,' Tirrell said.

I have spent far too much of my life being pushed around by my seniors and reluctantly pushing around my subordinates. Nowadays, anyone wanting to resume pushing me around had better be quite sure of his powers and his readiness to use them. Authority, I had discovered, has no value if the opposition ignores it. 'I expect you would, but you're doomed to disappointment. Mr Kitts knows as much as I do, possibly more, and I also want a witness to what I say and don't say. Failing which, I'm not saying a word until my solicitor is present and very probably not then.'

The Inspector opened his mouth but Beth spoke first. 'And I'm coming too. My husband was invalided out of the army and he is still below par. I will be the judge of whether and for how long he is fit to be questioned. If you have any objection, he stays here until I can get hold of his doctor.' Her face and voice left no room for argument. She handed Sam to Isobel.

Beth's words, coming from one who looked like a delicate teenager rather than a guardian, had all the more force. The Inspector made a helpless gesture and turned away. He had slumped fractionally from his usually erect bearing. He was no longer a self-contained man, securely in command of his own little world. He was, his posture said, the plaything of forces beyond his control. I knew the feeling. He had my sympathy if not my co-operation.

Our dialogue with Inspector Tirrell must have been clearly audible in the sitting room through two open doors. The two men already there rose to their feet, but whether out of old-fashioned courtesy to Beth or to be ready in case of a violent attack by an infuriated member of the public I could not tell.

One, the taller and evidently the senior, had the face of a terrier trying to ignore the smell of Antimate. He led off before we had finished seating ourselves. Seven behinds exceeded the capacity of our suite and the terrier showed no signs of giving up his armchair. The younger newcomer brought forward a spare upright chair for himself and gestured to Sergeant Cox to do the same. He was fair haired, smooth-faced and, Daffy said later, 'rather dishy'. And he knew it.

Terrier frowned at me. 'You are making a mistake —' he began.

'One moment,' I said. 'I prefer to know who's ranting at me.'

Terrier's frown turned into a ferocious scowl. 'This is Superintendent Fossick,' Tirrell said quickly, 'and Inspector Grey.'

'Of the Fife and Kinross Constabulary?'

Tirrell shook his head at me warningly.

Terrier — Superintendent Fossick — decided to let my needling go by. 'I would like to suggest,' he said more mildly, 'that you're making a mistake.' His accent came from further south, somewhere in the English Midlands. 'In order to substantiate the truth of what you say, you and other witnesses should make your statements separately. If the statements agree on details they can be taken as true. It's a standard technique for verifying evidence and the best way to confirm your innocence.'

'It's also an ancient dodge for trying to catch people out contradicting each other,'

Henry said. 'We've nothing to hide. Just don't try to treat us as though we're either half-witted or guilty of something.'

There was a momentary pause during which the silence seemed ready to burst.

'Very well,' Fossick said stiffly. 'If that's the way you want it . . .'

'That's the way we're going to get it,' Henry said. He was not finishing the Superintendent's sentence for him. It was a statement in its own right.

As Fossick led us through the story so far, it was clear that he had read and digested our previous statements; but, when we came to the events of that day, he wanted every word and made sure that he got them. The one topic which we managed to avoid was the use of the tranquillizer dart in Miss Otterburn's backside. If she ever worked out what had caused her brief period of unconsciousness, she could bring an action; but we were certainly not offering any confessions. If the matter should ever come to court, I had an uncomfortable feeling that the fact that Miss Otterburn had gone down in very few seconds would be taken as proof that I had loaded the dart for something larger than a Labrador.

At the end, Fossick came back to Miss Otterburn's arrival at the Bothy. 'You're sure that he said "microfiche"?' he asked us.

Henry and I both expressed certainty. 'There was a time when I was quite familiar with the word,' Henry said. 'I recognized it the moment it was uttered.'

'I can't think of anything,' I said, 'which would sound even faintly similar and not be ridiculous in the context.'

'How big was the envelope?'

'About three inches by two,' Henry said. I thought back and agreed.

'Your refusal to allow a search of the house looks bad,' Fossick said.

'Not my refusal,' I said. 'My wife's. But a search would not have contributed in the least to proving our innocence. In point of fact, I never laid a finger on it and nor, I'm sure, did Mr Kitts, but if I had taken it there are a thousand ways I could have disposed of it. So from my point of view a search would have had nothing but nuisance value.'

'But it looks bad,' Fossick repeated.

'Why should that worry me?' I asked him. 'I know that I'm innocent. No court in the land would think otherwise on the basis of what you've got. Your opinion's of no concern to me. It is irrelevant.'

'You're wasting your time pursuing Mr Cunningham,' Henry said, at his most urbane. 'We did not go out microfishing. We hope that the whole truth will eventually emerge so that, in the matter of quarantine regulations, Mr Cunningham will be seen to be an innocent victim of somebody else's crime. Beyond that, your problems are your own. In fact, we are no more than concerned members of the public and you are our employees.'

Fossick's brows came down again and he pursed his lips. 'Everybody has an interest in something that might be turned into money,' he said harshly.

Henry gave an uninterested shrug. 'This is the first time that anybody has suggested to us that the microfiche might have a — ah — fiscal value. I suggest that you try Miss Otterburn. Or has she also vanished?'

'Miss Otterburn returned to her office and endeavoured to bluff it out. On your say-so, she has been taken into custody on a charge of assault; you'd better be able to back it up when the time comes. She is now out on bail and threatening legal reprisals against absolutely everybody.' The Superintendent smiled grimly.

'Three of us witnessed the assault and Spurway will be able to confirm it, when he comes round,' I said.

'Perhaps. If his memory is unimpaired and if he is not under the impression that one of you was responsible. Miss Otterburn denies striking the blow and she is adamant that she doesn't have the microfiche. We are inclined to believe her. For one thing, her boss, Mr Heatherington, is still demanding that we pull out all stops for its recovery, which suggests that he has not received an offer for its return, whether or not —'

Fossick broke off. There was the sound of another car outside. I thought that our driveway must be looking like a municipal car park. The 'dishy' Inspector Grey, who might be subordinate to Superintendent Fossick and no more than equal in rank to Inspector Tirrell, had no intention of lackeying while there was a mere sergeant present. At his nod, Cox put aside his notebook and went to the front door.

He came back followed by the daunting figure of Hector Tholess, who accorded us greeting in the form of a single nod to share between us. He looked more peevish than ever and he seemed to have lost a little weight without any improvement in his general appearance.

As a matter of elementary courtesy I got to my feet, as did the others except Beth, but I had no intention of giving up my comfortable seat on the settee to a politician for whom I nursed a particular dislike. Nor, I could see, had Henry. The policemen exchanged looks but, before the outranked Tirrell was obliged to offer his chair, Tholess took a stand before the dead fireplace, thereby establishing a dominant position in the room as Tirrell had at the Bothy. He loomed like a thundercloud.

'Well?' he said to Fossick. 'Bring me up to date. Have you recovered it?'

'Not yet, sir,' Fossick said. 'The girl had it but swears that she lost it again. When she came round from an unexplained fainting fit, she says that her clothing had been disarranged.'

Henry and I exchanged a glance. He gave a minute headshake.

'What about these people?' Tholess asked, managing to indicate Beth and Henry and me with no more than a flick of the eyes. 'Have you searched the place?'

To be fair, Fossick had the grace to look embarrassed. 'They won't permit a search and their lawyer's blocking us from getting a search warrant. Strictly speaking, we don't need a warrant; but we need good cause and we don't have it yet — not that a search would have had any useful function, they knew that we were coming and they made sure that we knew it. But they flatly deny even knowing that the microfiche had any value let alone setting hand on it. I have a feeling that the journalist may be our best bet.'

Tholess's bulldog face looked as though a bigger bulldog had beaten it to the biscuit. It reminded me of a mastiff I had once seen trying to pass a sharp splinter of bone along with yesterday's dinner. 'If you're right, he must be found and damn quick. How hard are you looking for him?'

'Hard enough,' Fossick said. 'We've traced some of his movements. He arrived at Ardunie village on foot and phoned for a taxi which took him to Cupar. What he did there we don't yet know. An hour later, he took another taxi back here. His car is still at the door and I have men back and front. Unless he turned around and left again almost immediately, he's still somewhere nearby.'

'Then that's why they don't want a search,' Tholess said triumphantly. 'Go and find him.' He looked straight at me for the first time. I could feel the heat of it. 'And as for you, you must have signed the Official Secrets Act in your time.'

The door opened. 'That's what I was waiting to hear,' said a new voice. Mike Coutts walked into the room. 'I wanted to be able to tell the world how far you were prepared to push it.'

Nine

The journalist had been out of sight and out of our minds until a few moments earlier. His arrival on cue produced a stunned silence while everybody waited for somebody else to set the ball rolling.

Under his arm Mike Coutts had an envelope, but much larger than the one we had glimpsed at the Bothy. He pushed a folded slip of paper into my hand. It was a cheque. 'That should take care of the damage to your car,' he said. 'Forgive me.'

His voice broke the stalemate. 'Arrest that man and take possession of the envelope,' Tholess boomed, very near the top of his voice.

'Go right ahead,' Mike told the Superintendent, 'if you want to make a bad scandal ten times worse. You should never have been drawn into trying to save a politician's reputation.' He moved forwards as he spoke until he reached the centre of the group and took his stand in front of the dead fireplace, forcing Hector Tholess to give ground.

For the first time, Fossick seemed unsure

of himself. 'I have been assured that this matter originated at Porton Down.'

'Assured by Mr Tholess? And that it was, no doubt, far too secret for even your ears?'

Tholess began a vigorous protest but a frown and a gesture from Fossick made him break off. 'In your own interests,' the Superintendent told him, 'you should let me hear what's said. I'm quite capable of arriving at a sound conclusion.'

With an effort, the politician restrained himself. He had turned a shade darker. He leaned back against the corner table. I was on the point of asking him to be careful, because the table was old and had never been intended to support such a weight, when we heard two of Beth's ornaments jingling together as the table trembled in response to a quiver in Tholess's big frame. He stood up quickly.

Mike had been looking drawn, but suddenly he smiled. 'Very unwise of Mr Tholess, giving that assurance. He should have remembered that almost every political scandal since the first rogue convinced a gullible public that they should place themselves unreservedly at his mercy has been dwarfed by the scandal over the lies the culprit told in trying to scrape earth over it. Think of Profumo. Think of Richard Nixon. I dare say that some of the early work may have been done at Porton Down but as you may know, Superintendent, a great deal of work happens at Porton Down which is quite unconnected with germ warfare.'

'And Mr Tholess certainly had no business invoking Special Branch to try and pull his nuts out of the fire,' Henry said.

Fossick jumped. 'What makes you think that we're Special Branch?' he asked cautiously.

'What else? You're not a Scot. Englishmen do turn up in the Scottish police forces, but not very often. Inspector Tirrell admitted that you were not from Fife and Kinross. We have a scandal with a politician involved. If you're not Special Branch you'd better identify yourselves.'

Tholess had been fuming on the fringe of the discussion, eager to take it over but deterred by repeated warning signals from the Superintendent. The night was cool but we had not lit the fire, yet he was beginning to sweat. 'There is no scandal and I am not involved, merely concerned,' he ground out. 'Give me that envelope.'

Mike held it behind his back. 'You're big enough to take it by force,' he said. 'Do that, in front of witnesses, if you want to. It would only help to verify the story without doing you a damn bit of good.

'When I left the Bothy — your car let me down, by the way, John, and I had to walk as far as Ardunie — I went straight to Cupar and found a business office where they had a microfiche copier and a fax machine. Before coming back here and spending the afternoon in your spare bedroom, using my mobile phone to the full, I faxed four copies of the whole set, one to my editor —'

Tholess rounded on Fossick again. 'If we must discuss this matter instead of getting on with the proper business of ensuring confidentiality, could we at least do so out-with the presence of all these people?'

'I wouldn't bother myself on that score,' Mike said cheerfully. 'The facts will be in tomorrow's papers. They're probably al-ready typeset. And you know how uptight everybody got when D Notices were used to protect private reputations. You could never get away with it today.'

'What's more,' Beth said, 'you'd be far too late. We could make a very good guess already as to what it's all about and so could half a hundred other people, I should think.'

Those were the first words that she had spoken since entering the room. They pro-voked a few seconds of absolute silence.

Mike laughed aloud. 'Go ahead, then,' he said. 'You may help to show Mr Tholess that his bubble's already burst.'

Superintendent Fossick had risen to his feet. He placed himself between Mike and the now seething politician. 'Yes, go on,' he said. 'It's high time somebody told me what the hell's really going on.'

Now that I came to think about it, I realized that I could, as Beth had said, make a good guess as to what was going on; but Beth is much quicker than I am to arrive at a conclusion clear enough to verbalize. We all looked at her.

Beth took hold of my hand. Speaking to a crowd of more than two people always makes her nervous. 'Obviously,' she said, 'it's rabies. The truly awful killer. That's why everybody wets themselves as soon as it's mentioned. There was quite a ballyhoo two or three years ago, when Cook and Simpson came out with a vaccine that was cheaper than anything on the market at the time. Countries where rabies is endemic would be able to afford wholesale immunization of people and domestic animals and also to immunize wild animals by distributing bait laced with the vaccine.'

'That's quite right,' Henry said. 'It was going to be the beginning of the end for the scourge of rabies. On top of which, Cook and Simpson could be expected to make a fortune for their shareholders, with jobs in Aberdeen and Glasgow as a by-product.'

Beth was nodding. 'But there was a report in *Dog Monthly* a few weeks ago about fresh outbreaks of rabies in Pakistan, Turkey and somewhere else. The article, I remember, suggested that the time was not yet ripe for considering doing away with quarantine.

'Noel Cochrane started his working life as a biochemist, so he knew what it was about. Then he was promoted into marketing and went out to India, "to open up the market" was how he put it. Then he got another promotion and came back to head office after which, we're told, battles were raging among the management team.

'Suddenly, a whole lot of things happened in quick succession. Noel was heading abroad and taking his dog with him. Our car, with his case and the dog in it, was stolen. And, next thing we know, people, all of them connected to Cook and Simpson, are chasing after Noel and knocking each other on the head in their hurry to get their hands on whatever he's carrying. One girl has died, so they're not playing games.

'Now,' Beth said earnestly, 'you may care to believe that Noel is an industrial spy who has made off with a secret formula for eradicating tapeworms — or the ultimate man-made bacteria for germ warfare. No doubt that's what Mr Tholess would like you to believe. But Noel Cochrane isn't the sort of man to play dirty and, anyway, I prefer the simple and obvious explanation which is usually the right one. And the simple and obvious explanation, the one that fits all the facts and not just a chosen few of them, is that Noel observed that the new rabies vaccine wasn't only cheaper than its predecessors; it was also less effective. I asked Isobel what that would mean and she said that, just as a small change in the fox population could make the difference between rabies spreading and not spreading, so a small reduction in the effectiveness of the vaccine could leave room for fresh outbreaks. Especially if people had become over-confident and politicians were too deeply involved to dare confess that they had bought trouble.

'So that's what I think happened. I think that Noel came back to this country and had a flaming row with his fellow managers. I can guess that some of them, including Noel, would have wanted to do the proper thing and withdraw the product until they'd corrected the process, while some of the others said that it would cost too much and it would be a confession of liability and all the things that management do say when they've got that sort of problem.' Beth paused for breath.

'If that's all you have to offer —' Fossick began.

'It must have gone a lot further than that,' Beth said, 'or Mr Tholess wouldn't be getting so uptight about it. I expect that that's all explained by what was on the microfiche,' she added, with devastating simplicity.

Tholess attempted a careless laugh which came out more like the yapping of a small dog, shockingly out of keeping with his large body and bulldog face. 'I congratulate the young lady on her imagination,' he said. 'But, really, what a load of poppycock! No such product gets on the market until it's been tested over and over again.' He paused and, preferring bluster to derision, slammed his fist down on the mantel, nearly dislodging it from the wall. 'Superintendent, this slanderous speculation must be stopped before it goes any further!'

Beth flinched in the face of so much raw force but she was still game. 'Isobel says that laboratory tests count for very little. It's trials in the field that give you the real facts.'

Superintendent Fossick was watching Mike Coutts, who was smilingly miming a round of applause. 'I add my congratulations to those of Mr Tholess,' Mike said. 'You're very close to the mark. There's a host of ramifications but, of course, there's no way that you could have known those.'

'Then let's have them out in the open,' said the Superintendent. 'Either there has or there has not been a political offence or a risk to national security. If there has, then it's my business. Otherwise not.'

'I hope you're not proposing to listen to

any more of this claptrap,' Tholess exploded. 'I'm certainly not. I'll see that this business gets contained at a much higher level. Come, Superintendent.'

'I'll hear this out and then come to my own decision,' Fossick said.

'You are putting your job on the line.'

'It has been there before,' Fossick said quietly.

Tholess seemed to regain some of his lost mass. 'Very well. If that's your attitude, I shall seek an interview with the Prime Minister in the morning. And then we'll see. I'll have your head on a silver tray, Superintendent, and your balls alongside.'

He left the house in a rumble of footsteps and a slamming of doors. We heard tyres moving down the drive.

The Superintendent turned to resume his seat but Mike had beaten him to it. Fossick remained standing. He seemed uncertain whether to resent the loss of the comfortable chair or to enjoy his prime position.

'We shall indeed see,' said Mike. 'Another of my faxes went to the Cabinet Office for the personal attention of the PPS to the Prime Minister, with certain salient paragraphs underlined. From the correspondence, it's clear that Mr Tholess, while he was Scottish Secretary, pressed for an early approval of test results which, to say the least, were open to several interpretations.

Later, when the company tried to dismiss reports of fresh outbreaks as exaggerated or the outbreaks as coincidental, Tholess blocked any moves towards investigation by government scientists.'

Henry stirred. 'There must be even more to it than that. Those actions might be taken as mere errors of judgment but well intended, aimed at preserving a national investment and the jobs that went with it. Politicians survive that sort of *faux pas* every day of the week. They hardly explain Tholess's present attitude of defensiveness bordering on panic, let alone his personal presence at the search for the dog, armed with a rifle.'

'I can vouch for that,' I said. 'He made it clear that he was ready to shoot first and argue about it afterwards. Anyone with a suspicious mind might wonder whether he wasn't hoping for an excuse to kill the dog before it could trigger the scandal and multiply it a hundredfold by developing rabies right here in Britain.'

'Anyone with an even more suspicious mind,' Henry said, '— one as suspicious as mine — might even be wondering whether he hadn't been hoping for an encounter with Noel Cochrane at which there might have occurred an unfortunate accident.'

'Pure speculation,' said Fossick, but there was no weight in his voice. He had half

frowned in sudden thought and then nodded involuntarily.

'As you suggest, Henry, there's more,'
Mike said. 'Your friend Cochrane had been
very thorough in his researches.' Mike
tapped the envelope. 'Tholess, while he was
Scottish Secretary, had early knowledge of
the new vaccine. His sister-in-law invested
heavily in Cook and Simpson shares, which
did very well when the firm scooped the
market in rabies prophylaxis. Soon after
the first adverse reports would have
reached him, and while he was trying to
stall any official investigation, she sold out
very profitably.'

During the pause that followed I heard
Inspector Tirrell draw in his breath. Sergeant Cox closed his eyes for a moment as
if in prayer. I thought that I would not like
to be in Tholess's shoes when the story
broke next morning.

'When you publish this story,' Beth said
gently, 'aren't you going to be doing just
what Henry said, damaging a national investment and sweeping away a lot of jobs?'

'I hope not,' Mike said. 'As a journalist, I
see my duty as being to expose the truth
and only in the most extraordinary circumstances to make judgments as to whether
the truth should be told. But I have a
source of information inside Cook and
Simpson who hints at fresh developments

and that this story may soon be old history.

'Cook and Simpson had tried to undercut the cost of human diploid cell vaccine by genetic engineering, but the rabies glycoprotein produced was only partially effective against certain strains of rabies. While they were still denying that there was a problem they were struggling to overcome it and I gather that a more refined product, at so little extra cost that the firm will be able to swallow the difference, will be ready for the market within the next month or two. They may have to fight to live down the scandal and retain their market position, but they can do it.

'However, it's quite clear from the correspondence that Mr Tholess knew nothing of all that at the time. And as you yourself pointed out, Mrs Cunningham, the story is in the process of breaking. If I don't print it, somebody else will.'

We fell silent. I had a clear mental picture of another parliamentary career disappearing down the plug-hole of history.

'Very well,' Fossick said at last. 'Assuming that all this is true, my remaining interest in the case is reduced.'

'In other words,' said Henry, 'you have to consider what action should be taken against Mr Tholess for misuse of police time — and Special Branch time in particular.'

The Superintendent looked pained. 'I

need only gather the facts. The decision, thankfully, will not be mine.' He looked at Tirrell. 'And such questions as who killed Harriet Williams are not my concern.'

'Nor mine,' Tirrell said cheerfully. 'Although, as with yourself it's my duty for the moment to gather up the facts. You've been very helpful,' he told Mike Coutts. 'Perhaps you can help some more. But if you stay, the rest is off the record.'

'Until you give me the nod,' Mike said. 'Agreed.'

Tirrell held out his hand. 'And I'll take those copies now.'

Mike handed them over.

'Very well.' Tirrell was scanning rapidly through the shiny photocopies while he spoke. 'I come back again to Mr Cochrane. The man who triggered the whole series of events. If his intention was to publish or threaten to publish the material in order to prevent further damage and risk to human life — then his actions were praiseworthy and possibly even legal, while it may be assumed that those of his pursuers were probably not. Definitely not, when theft and violence were used. On the other hand —'

'No other hands,' I said. 'I've known Noel Cochrane for some time and I'm certain that his motives would be of the best. He saw the firm's product as a genuine blessing which could free the Third World from the scourge of rabies. He also loved animals and I know that the sight of rabid dogs in India distressed him enormously. When rabies not only made a comeback in Africa and the East but threatened to break out again in Europe, he must have been appalled. I believe that his intention would have been to force the company to admit its fault, recall old stocks, replace them with the improved vaccine and pay compensation wherever it was due.'

'That could be a lot of money?' Tirrell suggested.

'A huge amount,' Henry said. 'It's been kept very quiet — which I suspect is some more of Mr Tholess's doing — but I hear that the first death for many years has occurred in Europe and more than a few in the East. Bear in mind that company executives and board members usually feel bound to favour their own shareholders — including themselves — above any injured customers. They would be desperate to cover up.'

'And so,' Tirrell said, 'If — and I'm only saying if — Mr Heatherington has assured the police that the phone call he received from Mr Cochrane demanded money for the return of this material . . . ?'

'I'd say that somebody is lying,' I said.

'There could be no doubt about that,' said the Superintendent. 'But who?'

242

'Did Mr Heatherington really say that about Noel?' Beth asked unhappily.

Inspector Tirrell pursed his lips and looked down at the book in which he had either been making notes or doodling.

'He won't tell you,' Henry said. 'We're left to draw our own conclusions. Mr Cochrane may have some difficult questions to answer — but no doubt he can answer them very satisfactorily,' he added quickly as Beth bristled with indignation. 'Meanwhile the Inspector, on behalf of his seniors on the CID side, is much more concerned over who killed Harriet Williams.'

'I really didn't think that there was any doubt about that,' Beth said. 'Miss Otterburn — our Miss Johnson — whacked Mr Spurway over the head with a lady's umbrella matching the one that Hannah saw Miss Williams carrying. You saw her do it.'

'That may have been a one-off event,' I said. 'I really can't envisage a woman, even as forceful-looking as Miss Johnson, making a habit of it. Blunt instruments simply aren't a woman's natural weapon.'

Beth gave a ladylike chuckle of amused contempt. 'John,' she said, 'you're an old-fashioned, sexist, chauvinist porker. With so many men still having gallant hang-ups about not hitting women, I can more easily imagine a woman hitting another woman than a man doing the same thing. Anyway, it was a woman's umbrella and Harriet Williams must have been carrying it already weighted. That surely makes it a woman's weapon.'

Inspector Tirrell had been watching and listening, his eyes moving from one to the other of us as he waited for admissions, revelations or a new slant. Now, with the argument in danger of stalling, he decided to give it a kick in the tail. 'One thing I can tell you,' he said. 'Miss Williams was not struck down with the umbrella. Quite a different weapon was used.'

'Well, what?' Beth asked.

'That, I am not allowed to tell you. Have patience and you will probably read about it in the newspapers in a day or two.'

'A fisherman's priest,' Mike Coutts said. 'I'm told that they found dried salmon scales in the poor girl's hair. I had a good look around the Bothy — without disturbing anything, Inspector, except for the purpose of helping Noel Cochrane — and there was a full set of salmon fishing gear, down to the flies and spinners, but there wasn't a priest. No angler with respect for his fish would go after salmon without the means to give it a merciful rap on the head.'

'How did you know about the salmon scales?' Tirrell asked indignantly. 'No, forget the question. I know that asking a journalist about his sources is a waste of breath. I'll say this much. It looks bad for your friend Noel Cochrane.'

'He was with us when the girl was struck down,' I pointed out.

'The Inspector refers to blackmail,' Henry said. 'Not the killing.'

'Either way,' I said, 'I don't believe it.'

The discussion limped along for a few more minutes without opening up new ground. Tirrell looked at his watch. 'It's high time we were going,' he said.

The Superintendent nodded and rose. 'I agree. These people will still be here if you have more questions for them in the morning.'

When the police presence had at last been removed, Isobel and the two girls joined us in the sitting room. While Beth brought them up to date I acted as barman, but the drinks were not received in the cheerful spirit that usually pervaded our 'lowsing time' gatherings.

'That man Tirrell,' Beth wound up, 'doesn't believe us. He thinks we're giving Noel a false alibi because we like him or in return for Noel covering up some awful breach of the quarantine regulations on our part.'

Through a silence punctuated by indignant little noises, Mike Coutts spoke. 'In justice to Tirrell,' he said, 'I'm afraid that our friend Noel Cochrane is not showing up

245

in a very good light. I didn't want to say this while the police were here because it would have homed them in on my source, but Mr Heatherington did indeed accuse Cochrane of attempting blackmail. What's more, he has produced a fax — typewritten, fortunately or unfortunately according to your point of view — with Cochrane's name on it as sender, demanding a hundred thousand for the return of the documents.'

'Noel would have to be remarkably simple to send such a thing when a phone call would have done just as well,' I said.

'People can be very foolish at times,' Mike said. 'Not that I accept the fax at face value. It bears the Cook and Simpson mailing room date-stamp for the right date, but that could easily have been added retrospectively.'

'Mr Cochrane seems to have stepped out of his league,' Henry said. 'He might just as well have attacked an elephant with a pointed stick.'

Several frantic days went by. For a while it seemed as though our old life of tranquil work and play would never return. Somehow we scrambled and struggled and muddled through. We kept up with the work of the kennels, not only keeping our inmates in the manner to which they had become accustomed but even progressing the training programme. All this between furnishing several different branches of the police with information, fingerprints and statements which did not contradict each other, arguing with the Divisional Veterinary Officer and the local authority over Jove's disappearance and recovery and fobbing off the press with a prepared statement drafted by Mike Coutts which said a lot without actually revealing anything. Most difficult of all was persuading the police to furnish corroboration that Jove's escape had been due to a criminal act by somebody quite unconnected with the firm.

And during this period, while each of us was feeling like a conjuror with one ball too many — in the air, I mean — we remembered Noel Cochrane in his bed of pain, wherever that might be. Beth made the first enquiries and spoke to several male voices that had never heard of him, then to several more who had heard of him but had no idea where he was. When at last she tracked him down — he had been removed to Ninewells Hospital in Dundee — she was again blocked, this time by a female voice which admitted to knowing all about Noel but flatly refused to disgorge any of that precious information.

I took the phone away from Beth by brute force. It should not be the way of the world, but sometimes a man's voice conveys more authority. 'Who am I speaking to?' I asked.

The voice decided that that much information might safely be released. 'Ward Sister Lightbody.'

I tried to inject matching firmness and self-importance into my voice, together with just a trace of masculine appeal. If she imagined that she could smell testosterone over the phone line, so much the better. 'I want to know how Mr Cochrane is progressing.'

'Are you a relative?'

'I'm his brother.' Beth, who is the most truthful person alive, gave a disapproving headshake.

There was a pause. 'He didn't mention a brother as next-of-kin.'

I thought swiftly and played for time. 'Who did he mention?'

There was a rustle of paper over the line. 'That bit seems to have been left blank.'

'Blank,' I said, relieved. 'That describes me exactly. Noel always said so. How is he?'

The Ward Sister decided to unbend a little. 'He's suffered some bad contusions — that means bruises,' she added kindly. 'And three of his ribs are cracked. He was passing a little blood when he was brought here. The doctors were concerned. But that has now stopped and his scan was clear. They're fairly satisfied that there's no organic damage but they'll want to keep him under observation for another day or two.'

'That's excellent,' I said. 'May I speak to him?'

'The police aren't allowing any visits or phone calls yet.' She paused again and then, curiosity triumphing over discipline, decided to let her hair down the rest of the way. 'What on earth has he been up to?' she asked.

'His girlfriend's husband caught up with him,' I said. Sometimes my tongue runs away with me.

'Then why are the police so interested in him?' she asked suspiciously.

'He's the head of the Mafia in Auchtermuchty,' I told her. She rang off indignantly.

'You'd better make any further calls,' I told Beth.

She nodded, frowning in reproof. 'All men are liars,' she said, 'but sometimes you take the cake.'

I was fairly sure that the police had no business holding Noel incommunicado without bringing any charge against him, but I decided that to rush in and invoke an army of lawyers might provoke exactly the reaction that Noel least wanted.

Masterly inactivity proved to be the correct choice.

Mike Coutts had returned to the newspaper office in Glasgow. He continued to prove himself as good as his word. In view of the various legal actions pending, his preliminary articles could only hint at the various acts of violence committed in pursuit of Noel and his microfiche; but he went to town on the subject of the rabies vaccine and Hector Tholess's part in that unsavoury story. And he was free to recount the theft and destruction of my car with the release of Jove, so that his readership was left in no doubt that we had been taken unawares by the theft and had recovered the dog with little aid from the authorities. The likelihood of public sympathy undoubtedly tempered the attitudes of the authorities in their dealings with us.

On the Sunday, the day after our abortive chat with the ward sister, Mike returned in the hope of further news and for a social visit to Jove with whom he had struck up a rapport. Mike had also tracked Noel as far as Ninewells and, like us, had so far failed to make any closer contact.

We had made one further attempt to reach Noel by phone, only to find that the ward telephone trolley was in such regular use by patients summoning their transport home that there were heavy odds against it being free at the moment of any given incoming call. Beth had left our phone number with a message inviting Noel to phone us. Remembering what I had told her of Noel's state when hospitalized, she guessed that he might not have any money with him and added that he could call us and reverse the charges. The ward sister, if that was she, retorted huffily that they had a telephone fund in aid of impoverished patients, to which we might care to contribute.

Either the message or the telephone trolley may have been slow to reach Noel, by which time I was busily engaged on the lawn, with Mike an interested conscript to help me. One of the pups just entering serious training had got it firmly into his head that any version of the Stop-and-sit command really meant Come-back-here-and-sit. (This can be one of the trickiest faults to cure, because the very last thing to be taught is Don't-come-back.) Mike was handling the check-lead while I laboured with voice and whistle and hand signals and telepathic commands of increasing intensity, when the cordless phone in my pocket began its ramped signal.

I switched the phone from 'Receive' to 'Talk' and said 'Hello.'

'Can you be overheard?' Noel's voice asked.

Not only could I have been overheard by anyone near the house or in the road beyond the garden wall, but cordless phones are seriously insecure — as certain noble personages have found to their cost. 'Hold on,' I said. I called to Hannah to take over the pup and we went indoors. I picked up the kitchen phone, making sure that the cordless instrument — which would otherwise have been broadcasting our conversation to anyone interested enough and equipped to listen in — was switched off before speaking again.

'Secure at this end,' I said. 'How about you?'

'Should be all right. I'm in a side ward, courtesy of BUPA. Did you phone up yesterday?'

'Yes.'

'I didn't know you were my brother. Dad certainly got around.'

'They never disclose medical information except to close relatives,' I explained. 'We wanted to know how you were. So how are you? You sound a great deal perkier than I expected.'

'I still feel as though I've been trampled by elephants, but they aren't quite such oversize elephants as they were yesterday. By tomorrow they may be down to mere elephant size.' Noel's voice lost its bantering note and became serious. 'Listen, will you do me a favour? I know you've already done me a bigger one than I can repay. I'm told that you rescued me when otherwise I would probably have been knocked off or left to die in that chest. I won't even try to thank you; these things are beyond words. But I need a little more help and I can't think of anyone else I can trust.'

'You don't have to go on about it,' I said. 'You only have to ask.'

Although he had said that he was alone, he lowered his voice. 'I want something fetched from the Bothy.'

I tried to keep every trace of amusement out of my voice. 'If it's what I think it is, I have it here.'

'And if that's what I think it is,' he said gruffly, 'I'll be very glad to have it; but that's not my prior concern at the moment. Can you go to the Bothy for me and collect every scrap of paper that's been left behind? That bloody Tirrell admits that they didn't bother too much about gathering it all up and he says his men are too busy to run errands for me, but he says they've finished with the Bothy now and he'll release the keys to you for the purpose of collecting my property only, which includes certain scraps of paper.'

'Are you looking for any particular piece of paper?' I asked him. 'Or just starting a do-it-yourself salvage operation?'

'I'd rather not talk about it on the phone,' Noel said. 'Just every scrap of paper. And I'll have to ring off now. Rounds have just finished and another dozen lucky buggers are busting to phone for their lifts home. They're gathering outside the door and glaring in at me. Thanks. You've taken a weight off my mind. I'll look for you later today.' And either he hung up without waiting for any more assurances or somebody pulled out the plug.

While I was on the phone, Isobel and Daffy between them had put a hot snack on the kitchen table. Henry drove over in time to share it with us. While we ate — all eight of us, including Sam who was as usual on Beth's knee and greedily accepting something special — I gave the others a summary of my talk with Noel.

Beth must have recognized irritation in my voice. 'And you hate wasted journeys,' she said sympathetically.

'I hate wasted anything,' I said. 'That's probably why I didn't go higher than captain in the army — I was always up in arms about the logistical wastefulness of it all. There was a total comprehension gap. I couldn't see why my superiors didn't plan things out properly in advance instead of sending everybody and everything all over the world and back to where they came from; but those superiors looked on that as being my blind spot rather than theirs.'

My partners and the staff always humoured my little foibles. 'Let's see if we can help,' Daffy said. 'The Bothy's west of here, Mr Cochrane's in Ninewells which is generally north, but the key has to be fetched from Cupar, which is to the south.'

'One moment,' Beth said. She handed Sam to Hannah and took the cordless phone out into the hall.

'I can save you one trip,' Daffy said. 'The owner of that daft setter phoned. She's back at home, but only because her car was wrecked and she's got a busted ankle. She says it was entirely that other driver's fault but I'd like to hear his side of it. She offered the equivalent of the taxi fare if we'd deliver her darling Rufus to her. I said I'd ask you and call her back this afternoon. She lives just beyond Ardunie. I could take your car, broken window and all, deliver the dog and visit the Bothy on the same journey.'

'If it's any help,' Mike Coutts said, 'I want to see Noel Cochrane. I could take you over.'

'And I could fetch all the toffee papers and used tissues to you at Ninewells,' Daffy said helpfully, 'and bring you home again.'

Beth came back into the room and re-claimed Sam. 'Inspector Tirrell has a car coming to the village. He's sending the keys of the Bothy to the local cop-shop. One of us can collect it from there.'

'And if you like,' Daffy said, 'I could take the papers direct to Mr Cochrane and save you going anywhere at all. You could stay here and get on with things.'

But I refused the offer. I had something for Noel and he would never have forgiven me for delegating that particular delivery, especially to Daffy.

'It seems to work out very neatly,' Henry said. 'Give my regards to Noel Cochrane. I would come with you, except that I'm expecting a phone call from my nephew in the States. Just in case of hiccups, you'd better borrow this.' He handed his mobile phone to Daffy. 'You and Mr Coutts should exchange mobile numbers. These complicated arrangements have a habit of breaking down.'

'So have the simple ones,' I said. 'But I think the time of emergencies is over for now.'

Ten

Mike Coutts's big car bore all the signs of being a hard-worked tool of the trade to a man whose trade necessitated getting from A to B frequently and in a hurry. The interior was untidy and as scuffed as the outside. From the registration letter it could not have been more than eighteen months old at the most, but when I looked at the dash I saw that it had already racked up a mileage which, straightened out, would have taken him around the world. But it was quiet and comfortable and, as we crossed the Tay Estuary by the toll bridge and wafted up the Riverside to the low concrete mass of Ninewells Hospital, I enjoyed the luxury of being driven for a change and being free to admire the changing views of water and hills.

After several enquiries and more than a little walking, we found Noel's side-ward. I left Mike Coutts out of sight and earshot while I went in, explaining that I wanted a word in private with Noel. Mike probably thought that I was priming Noel with what to tell him.

Noel was reclining against pillows. He had changed colours as his bruises worked their way along the spectrum, but he was evidently on the mend. He wore hospital pyjamas and a woollen hat borrowed from some Dundee United supporter.

'This is instead of fruit,' I said, handing over a small carrier bag.

He leaned up on his elbow and peered inside. The bag contained his toupee, which I had rescued from the Bothy, together with his sticky tape, a small pair of scissors and a comb.

'Thanks,' Noel said huskily. 'You're a pal. I don't really go much of a bundle on fruit. What about the other thing?'

'Daffy's gathering up the bits of paper now,' I told him. 'She'll bring it over to us when she's got it all. If you wouldn't mind a visit from Mike Coutts, I'll go and fetch him. It will take me several minutes.'

Noel understood precisely. 'I want to see him very much . . . in a few minutes' time.'

I rejoined Mike Coutts and explained that we would have to wait because Noel was getting a blanket bath. We chatted about nothing for a while. Then two nurses came past. Nurses are sometimes homely, but these two were young, blonde, leggy and at that perfect stage of womanhood when the bloom of youth overlaps the knowledge of sexual magnetism. They were smiling at some shared joke.

'Ah! He'll be ready for us now,' I said.

Mike seemed thoughtful as he followed me to the side-ward. I hoped that the upward leap of Noel's image might be reflected in print. I took a quick look round the door to be sure that Noel was ready. The woollen hat was out of sight and Noel was once again crowned with his mop of curly brown hair. Despite the bruises, he could hardly have been recognized as the man in the wooden chest. 'Mike!' he said. 'I've been wanting to see you.'

The two shook hands. 'And here I am. How are you?'

'Mending. That bastard worked me over more than once. Do you have the story?'

'Most of it. I'd like to hear your version of it, but you needn't compromise your integrity by talking to the press unless you want to clarify a few motives.' Noel hesitated but Mike rolled on. 'You can correct me if I go off the rails. Your employers were deep into rabies vaccines at prices even the Third World, where most of the world's rabies is still endemic, could afford. During your time in India, you discovered that, for some reason we needn't go into now, the products were less effective than the firm was claiming, to the point that fresh outbreaks could occur and people who thought that they were protected might be in great danger.

You must have been horrified.'

'More than horrified,' Noel said. His eyes looked old and tired and I could see again a trace of the man in the wooden chest. 'I can't think of a strong enough word. You see, I'd had a hand in developing the new vaccine. I felt responsible for all the death and disease that might follow.'

Mike nodded and went on. "When you returned to Britain, you found that your reports had been noted and believed but that the firm had no intention of doing anything about it while the money-tree was still fruiting.'

'It was bad,' said Noel, 'but not as bad as you make it sound. Partly, I'd like to think wholly, the reasoning was that to withdraw the vaccine before the replacement was ready would be an admission of liability. Off the record . . . ?'

'If you say so.'

'Off the record, what really stuck in my gullet was that Heatherington and the chief finance officer had done a discounted cash flow of forecast profits against probable costs in lawsuits and compensation. That's what really made me act.'

'And you acted to some effect,' Mike said. 'You raided the computer and other files and made off with a microfiche of some very damaging documents. True so far?'

'No comment,' Noel said.

'Which means yes.' Mike looked at Noel with sympathy and, I thought, even pity. 'Get wise,' he said. 'From the moment of your . . . defection, you were being hunted by colleagues and others who were quite prepared to step outside the law. Stolen cars were the least of it. The shit is now in process of hitting the fan and any of your pursuers who want to lessen its effect are going to swear blind that you were trying to blackmail the firm. Showing you in a bad light can only make them look better by contrast and, if they get brought to court, give their advocates a forceful argument in mitigation.'

'Believe me, I'm aware of that,' Noel said grimly.

'Are you also aware that a fax has been produced, ostensibly from yourself, demanding a large sum of money for the return of those documents instead of their delivery into my hands?'

'No, I wasn't,' Noel said. 'It's a fake.'

'But can you prove it? And can you prove what the others were after?'

Noel shrugged. 'It seems that I'm going to have to play as dirty as the rest. You'll give me a fair break?'

'Guaranteed.'

'Not attributable to me?'

'It will have less effect,' Mike said.

'All the same. When the dust settles, I

may still have a place in the firm. I know that some of the board members were on my side.'

'All right, then,' said Mike.

'But knowing and proving may be streets apart. Beginning with Uncle Joe —'

'Who?' Mike demanded. 'Your uncle . . . ?'

Noel shook his head violently and then blinked as the movement sent aches through his injuries. 'Old Man Heatherington. He's known as Uncle Joe after Joe Stalin, because if you disagree with him you're not likely to be seen around head office for much longer. The snag to that way of working is that when things go wrong the autocrat has to carry the whole can.'

'I can see that he'd be desperate to cover up,' Mike said. 'But his secretary, Miss Otterburn alias Johnson. Is she so loyal?'

'She hates his guts. She's a very hard nut. If she has a soft spot . . .'

'Donald Aggleton?' I said.

Noel looked surprised. 'Whatever gave you that idea?'

'She suggested it herself. Was it another lie?'

'You remember Donald?' Noel asked Mike.

'He met us for drinks some evenings,' Mike said. 'Your assistant, wasn't he?'

'He had a thing going with Kate Otterburn for years. They had ideas above their incomes. They took on a mortgage to buy a mansion of a house in Bellshill and then struggled to find the money to get the dry rot and woodworm out of it. They were full of mad schemes to raise money. Donald knew what was going on with the rabies vaccine and my views about it. If they saw a chance to cash in, they'd leap at it. But they broke up about a year ago and she ended up in possession of the house. She'd still be hungry for money to restore it. And she left him broke.'

'And Harriet Williams?'

Noel's face changed. 'Yes. Poor Harriet. I think that in her heart of hearts Harriet agreed with the stand I was taking. But she was an ardent feminist and a victim of driving ambition.'

'A dangerous combination,' Mike said.

'It can be. It was, with Harriet. She wanted to prove to the world that a woman's as good as a man or better. Which may be perfectly true,' said Noel thoughtfully. 'I wouldn't know. It seems to me that nature played some dirty tricks on women and just as many different ones on men. But Harriet seemed to think that the fact that Mother Nature — traditionally a female figure, note — decreed that women need not be physically as strong as men, but could instead look to men for support and protection, was a deliberate and malicious act on the part of the male sex. One hint that recovering those documents might lead to promotion into my job and she'd have been off and running!'

Mike was not taking notes. I wondered whether he was wired for sound, trusting to a first-class memory or only gathering background material. From the effort showing around his eyes, I guessed that he was memorizing. 'That leaves Jake Spurway,' he said. 'Mr Heatherington's personal hard man and fixer. According to Miss Otterburn-Johnson, he'd turned his coat and gone into business for himself, which is why Mr Heatherington set a pair of rather ineffective toughs on the trail. She claimed that she was still providing the romance in Donald Aggleton's life and she wanted the warning message passed to him. That right, John?'

'More or less,' I said hesitantly. Mike looked at me sharply. 'You've correctly quoted the statements she made to us. We decided later that she was trying to warn Donald Aggleton off. But according to Miss Laidlaw it was Harriet Williams who was sweet on Donald Aggleton.'

'You've been onto Madge have you?' Noel asked. 'I wouldn't rely too much on her news. She was always inclined to sniff romance where none existed and she was usually several years out of date. Kate Otterburn had come into and gone from Donald's

264

life for many a long month.'

Mike paused and pinched his upper lip, apparently as a help to thought. 'That seems to add up. So let's take it that Jake Spurway really had turned his coat. With what in mind?'

'Blackmail, I should think,' Noel said.

'That seems possible. Now let's have your story . . . from the theft of John's car onward.'

'For comparison purposes? You don't trust anybody, do you?'

'No,' Mike said frankly, 'I don't. Not when I've got to make up my mind whose side I come down on in print. If I get it wrong I lose my reputation and get sued for libel.'

'By me? I suppose that's perfectly possible,' Noel said. 'How much are you good for?' He was trying not to smile — because, I think, smiling still hurt his face.

'Don't get any big ideas. You went with John to see the burning car?'

'As soon as John said that it wasn't his car,' said Noel, 'I became no more than a bystander as far as the police were concerned. They let me tag along and I recognized the body as being Harriet. That, you may guess, shook me right down to my socks.'

'You never let on,' I said.

'How could I? The police wouldn't have let me out of their sight for days. I still had the microfiche on me. I was ready to cut and run. But I wanted my dog and I was damned if I was going to run off and leave him to be shot as an escapee from quarantine. I went to Myresie and took a room for the night. I wanted to be alone to think it over. You may guess that I didn't sleep much that night. By morning, I'd decided that I could trust John to look after Jove's interests, probably better than I could.'

'Your faith seems to have been more than justified,' Mike said.

I thanked them both.

'Not at all,' Noel said politely. He looked at Mike. 'So I decided to phone John, tell him that I was leaving Jove's fate in his hands, and beat it.

'But the pub didn't have a phone where I wouldn't have been overheard by the landlord, his staff, the other guests and even by passers-by in the street. Before I could find a safer phone I heard about another estate car being found dunked in the Tay at Lindhaven. At the pub, I was told that the only taxi in the village was away for its MOT test and not expected to pass; but a salesman, the only other person stopping over at the pub, said he was going through Lindhaven and that there was a taxi at the garage there.

'So I took a lift with him. Just short of Lindhaven I spotted what I thought looked like your travelling boxes near the road so I got out there and let my lift go. When I walked round the bushes to take a good look at the boxes — I was whistling for Jove as I went, I remember — I saw Donald Aggleton lying on the ground. I bent over him to see if he was still breathing — he was and I'm told that he still is. Then a rug came down over my head and I was trussed up like a turkey in about ten seconds flat.'

'We must have missed you by minutes,' I said.

Mike was frowning. 'You didn't see a car?'

'Not at that stage. I heard a car drive up shortly afterwards.'

Mike's frown cleared. 'Driven by Miss Otterburn?'

Noel shook his head carefully. 'I never saw her, or heard her voice.'

'Let's get this straight,' Mike said. 'It was Jake Spurway who gave you a hammering?'

'More than one hammering,' said Noel. 'And no, it wasn't Jake.'

'But he told Miss Otterburn —' Mike began. 'No, come to think of it, he didn't, if John relayed his words correctly.'

'He certainly implied it,' I said.

'That's right. Well, if he didn't, who did?'

'Jake talks a good game,' Noel said. 'In point of fact, he's a fairly good security man. The really tough cookie's his assistant.'

Mike looked stunned.

I remembered Henry's report of Miss Laidlaw's information. 'Spragg,' I said.

'Harry Spragg,' Noel confirmed. 'I told the police about him. My God! Haven't they got him?'

'I'd have heard if they had,' said Mike.

'Then all and sundry had better watch their backs. Spurway put up the better front but Spragg was the natural leader of the two of them in toughness and general villainy, though he preferred a background role. It was Spragg who was determined to make me cough up my evidence and he didn't give a damn how permanent was the damage he did.' Noel raised his chin. 'But he never broke me. I was more determined than he was. And I had more to lose.'

'Apparently,' Mike said. 'But why was that? We come now to the crunch question. Can you prove that you were on the side of the angels?'

Noel smiled grimly. 'I bloody well hope so,' he said. 'That's why I wanted the paper from the Bothy. The only document I hadn't transferred to the microfiche, because it was last of all, was a copy of the genuine fax I sent to Uncle Joe, certified by the solicitor whose office I sent it from. It demanded a withdrawal of all the faulty stock, its replacement by equal stocks of the earlier, better products at no greater cost, and an information pack to the WHO. Spragg came across it in my briefcase but he only glanced at it, saw that it wasn't what he was after at the time and ripped it up and across. The police have the rest of it but a vital quarter is still missing.'

'You didn't have the solicitor keep a copy?' Mike asked.

'Hell, no! At that time, I still looked on myself as a loyal member of the company. For that matter, I still do. I was trying to reach a satisfactory compromise without making a scandal. I didn't even let the solicitor read the document. I made him hold it, upside down, and certify it as the original of the fax which his secretary was sending on my behalf.'

'Then you'd better pray that it turns up.'

'Believe me, I am.'

I had been growing uneasy. 'Did the fax which was sent include that endorsement?' I asked.

Noel paused for a moment. 'I think so,' he said. 'The solicitor signed it and then it was sent off. Why?'

'Because I think that you two are missing one important point,' I said. 'That fax isn't just important for proving Noel's good intentions. Think about it. In turn, it also brands everybody else who came chasing after your microfiche as intending to make criminal use of it, because if you, Noel, were acting with the best intentions, anyone try-

269

ing to frustrate you had to be acting with the worst; above all, of course, it shows up Uncle Joe — Mr Heatherington — as a liar attempting to pervert the course of justice by fabricating evidence. Now that it's all coming out into the light of day, Uncle Joe and others, who anyway knew that there had to have been an original of the fax, will be much better placed if they can get their hands on that original, destroy it and pass off their version as the one true writ. It may not be a defence, but it would, as Mike said, make a forceful argument in mitigation.'

'It wouldn't mitigate murder,' Noel said.

'It might go a long way towards it if they could also argue that death was not intended,' I said. 'Somebody is killed but only moderate violence was meant. If that death occurred as part of a criminal action it would be classed as murder and everybody involved would be tainted by it. If it occurred, possibly by accident, during a well-intended effort to recover confidential papers being used for purposes of blackmail . . . think for a moment about the different view a court might take of it.'

'Would Uncle Joe see that?' Mike asked Noel.

Noel was looking ashen. 'Uncle Joe doesn't miss a thing,' he said. 'And Harry Spragg is still on the loose. Mike —'

'I'm ahead of you.' Mike handed me his

mobile phone. 'You'd better warn that weird-looking young woman.'

I keyed in the number of Henry's phone. To my great relief, Daffy answered almost immediately.

'Where are you?' I asked her.

'At the Bothy.'

'You'd better finish up very quickly and get the hell away from there,' I said. 'Others may come looking for bits of paper, and they won't be friendly. Be ready to run like a rabbit.'

'Okey dokey.' Daffy sounded, as usual, quite unperturbed.

'Just a moment.' Noel held out his hand and I passed the phone to him. 'Er — Daffy, is it? Have you finished looking?'

'As finished as I'll ever be,' Daffy said. Noel held the instrument slightly away from his ear. I could hear her words, faint but clear.

'Have you found a torn part of an A4 sheet of typing paper with my writing on it? It's —'

'I know your handwriting,' Daffy said. 'It's bloody awful, worse than a doctor's. I have something here that could be it. As near as I can make it out, the beginning reads, "It is with great reluctance," then there's a bit missing, then something about "common humanity" —'

'That's it,' Noel almost shouted. 'Keep it safe, but go, go, go.'

There was a pause. 'I think it's too late,'

Daffy said. 'There's a car pulling up outside. I'm going to hide myself away.'

I grabbed the phone. 'They'll know you're there by my car's presence.'

'I left your car in a track. I think it's where you parked last time. I mistook your route and turned too soon, so it seemed easier to cut through the trees. Got to switch off now. Bye.'

Noel grabbed the phone again. 'Keep yourself safe,' he said quickly. 'And keep that page even safer.' But the phone was dead.

Eleven

I took back the phone. My mind was racing without going anywhere.

'It could be somebody perfectly innocent,' Noel said hopefully. 'Dog-walkers or bird-watchers or something similar.'

My mind clicked into gear. I shook my head. The arrival had come too pat. 'We can't chance it,' I said. The phone in Daffy's hands would be dead but even if it had still been switched on I would not have been able to call her without betraying her chosen hidey-hole. And if I dialled the emergency services from Ninewells I would come up in Dundee and there would be endless questions before anyone would relay a message to Fife. I keyed in my own number. Henry's voice answered.

'Daffy's at the Bothy,' I told him. 'She has visitors and they're probably hostile. Can you get on to the police at Cupar and get them to send somebody? Quickly?'

Henry was nobody's fool. 'Can do,' he said. The line went dead.

I was looking for reassurance. 'What sort of man would attack a girl like Daffy?' I

273

asked the world in general.

'A brave one,' Mike said. Remembering Daffy's get-up for the day, leaning heavily on black leather and metal studs, I hoped that he might be right.

'A man like Harry Spragg,' Noel said grimly.

The day was Sunday. Smaller, local police stations would be unmanned and the few officers on duty would be out dealing with firearms certificates or traffic problems. There might be no urgent response to such a vague alarm. We would be no less in touch in the car. 'Let's go,' I said to Mike.

'Keep me posted,' Noel called after us.

We hustled through the long corridors, unsettling the throngs of visitors with their flowers in polythene and fruit in baskets. Mike had to bully his way out of the car park and onto the service road. The big car took the 'sleeping policemen' in its stride. Ahead I could see the low hills of Fife. I could make out the line of the through road and could almost pick out the Bothy, but a broad river lay between.

Mike swept us through the thin traffic and round the Riverside at a speed that made my stomach curdle. He said later that he was quite prepared to ignore any police interference in the hope of bringing a trail of police cars with us. But the police, that day, were elsewhere.

I had money ready. As we slowed at the tollgate I leaned across Mike, and then we were away again and hurling ourselves across the Tay Road Bridge. Mike's phone, which was still in my pocket, began to sound.

It was Henry. 'Your friend Tirrell's off duty,' he said. 'They're sending a car but the duty inspector wants you to call him and give more details, plus detailed directions for finding the place.'

Henry gave me a Kirkcaldy number and disconnected. I keyed the number. The duty inspector sounded young and unsure of his powers. I gave him directions for finding the Bothy before we ran into the area of heavy interference under the radio mast at the Fife end of the bridge and the connection was broken off. I decided not to renew it just yet. Keeping my eyes open and retaining control of my bowels was quite enough effort without trying to verbalize the situation to a disbelieving officer while Mike took the shortest route and slashed through Newport and Wormit. He had made his turn towards Perth and was ripping along the unclassified road which twists and turns towards Newburgh above the Tay, when the phone, still in my hand, woke up again. I answered it.

A voice which I had hoped for but not dared to expect whispered in my ear.

'Daffy?' I said.

Mike slowed down to a mad rush.

'I got out through a window,' she said softly. 'Can you hear me?'

'Yes.'

'Can't speak any louder, I think they're looking for me. I'm trying to get back to your car.'

I gestured to Mike to get a move on. 'The police are on the way,' I said. 'And we can be there in about fifteen minutes. More like ten,' I added as Mike put his foot firmly down again. 'Maybe less. If you get clear, watch for Mr Coutts's car.'

I received no direct answer from Daffy. 'Oh, shit!' said her voice.

'Daffy?' I said. 'Daffy?' But the line was dead.

Mike went through a dip and blind bend in one long slither, still picking up speed.

I sat rigid with tension for the last few miles. When the village of Ardunie was breaking the skyline half a mile ahead, Mike slowed for the turning into the by-road towards the Bothy. My heart may not have been in my mouth — a literal impossibility — but there was certainly a major obstruction in my gullet. Daffy was entitled to many years of laughter and loving. Her life added colour to ours by her very eccentricity. She was a friend, a worker and a topic of sometimes scandalized discussion. Without her

. . . no, it was, had to be, inconceivable.

In my anxiety, I nearly missed the one, crucial sight. I took a second look past Mike's head and a third. I could produce only an inarticulate croak. Then I recovered my voice and I was shouting at Mike to make a right. Mike braked hard and slid. We were almost on top of the insignificant junction.

'What?' Mike said. He slewed his car into the track. It was more than a ninety degree turn but he held the skid and pumped the throttle again.

'That's my car . . .' I said.

It was clear that history had repeated itself. My car had again been starved of fuel by the anti-thief device, had conked out in much the same place and, while the car was still rolling, the driver had seized his chance to swing off into the same farm track as Mike had chosen, and stopped in the same open space beside the upturned tine harrow. A blue Granada estate was parked nose to tail with my new car and both tailgates were open.

Mike stamped on his brakes. Downhill on dirt, the car slid, gripped and slid again, and came to a halt a few yards short of the Granada which, I noticed, was wearing the number-plates from my old car.

The human figures resolved themselves. A man and a woman were pulling another out of the back of my car. The other was Daffy. Her hands seemed to be fastened behind her. The woman was Catherine Otterburn.

We were out of Mike's car almost before it had settled back on its springs.

There was no hope of discussion. The couple were already beyond reasoning. Aggression was open. War had already been declared. Daffy was dropped, forgotten.

The Amazon came at me, swinging a sawn-off pick-handle. I stepped back and felt the wind of her first violent swing against my cheek. She swung back, determined to knock my head over the furthest trees, and again I had to dodge.

She was making no attempt to protect herself, confident either in the effect of her blow or in the reluctance of a man to hit a woman. But I had served in Northern Ireland, where a woman who had been carrying guns hidden in a perambulator on behalf of a terrorist hit-squad, understandably resenting her arrest, had come at me with a knife and but for the quick action of my sergeant I might well have been nearly filleted.

So I had no inhibitions about defending myself. I caught her between swings, grabbed her wrist with my left hand and with the other I jabbed with straight fingers up below her breasts. The club went flying and I held her by both wrists but in seconds she was recovering her breath and I had the proverbial tiger by the tail.

The business-like Miss Otterburn was as athletic as she had looked. Half winded, she was still a hissing, swearing, struggling bundle of elbows, fingernails and heels. In self-defence I pulled her to me, face to face, and gripped her wrists behind her back. She was not tall enough to reach my jaw with her head or my throat with her teeth — she tried both — and she was too close to kick me in the groin.

During the few seconds that our tussle had lasted I had been half aware of activities outwith our tiny arena. While another car braked hard on the nearby road, making a great hullabaloo, there had been a flurry of activity between Mike and the man. Now I took in that Mike was sitting and nursing his jaw and that the man had retrieved the sawn-off pick-handle. He was middle-aged but wiry, and from the harsh angles of his face I would have doubted that he had ever smiled in his life. In his movements I read absolute confidence in his own violence. He knew for a fact that he would triumph as he had in the past; and that piece of knowledge tends to be self-fulfilling. Moreover, it seemed that I could not count on any help from Mike Coutts. If I released my hold on Miss Otterburn I would be outnumbered and if I did not he would have me at his mercy. I picked her up by the waist, preparing to use her as a shield or a club and deciding that my best bet would be to hit the man with the woman, kick them both where it would hurt most and run for it.

Almost casually, as if trying it for size, he swung at me with the club. I jerked the woman off her feet and swung her round. If her partner happened to knock her brains out, that would leave me with only one to deal with. But the blow only parted her hair so that she screamed. The man nodded to himself and changed his grip.

There was a limit to how long this could last. I braced myself to throw the woman into his next swing.

We had both reckoned without Daffy, who was in such a state of fury that a trifle like having her hands still tied behind her was as nothing. She had struggled with difficulty to her feet. Now she dashed forward, leaped at the man and butted him. The sound of that clash of heads made me feel sick.

Cat-like, Daffy somehow landed back on her feet but the man was not so lucky. He was thrown two paces backwards. I saw the blood springing out on his face. Then he tripped and sat down hard, not on the ground but on one of the newly sharpened tines of the harrow.

The third car skidded to a halt nearby. I looked round just as it disgorged two uniformed policemen. I realized that part of the noise I had heard had been its klaxon.

Mike was getting shakily to his feet. 'I should have known better,' he said. 'The first rule of journalism is "Get near, get the story, but never get involved"!' He swayed and nearly fell.

The man was making a noise such as I had seldom heard before and then only on active service. I hope never to hear the like of it again. He was trying desperately to drag himself off the spike but without success.

The two policemen were very young. I know that that statement may be taken as implying that I was growing old, but they really were young. They were left in no doubt that the man was badly injured. One went to kneel beside him while the other, first carefully locking the police car which was blocking all chance of escape for any of the other cars, tried to take charge.

With the police more or less in control and no real hope of a rapid departure, Miss Otterburn stopped struggling and even began to relax. Daffy came to me to be untied but I kept my grip on the woman. God alone knew how she might react if I released her. She was a well-built girl and at another time the contact might not have been un-pleasant but at the moment I was more interested in recovering my breath. Daffy turned her back to Mike and held out her hands.

The kneeling policeman was using his personal radio to call for back-up and an ambulance. The other approached our small group. 'That man is badly injured,' he told me severely, as though quite sure that it was all my fault.

I was in no mood for being ticked off by a juvenile bobby. 'Serve him bloody well right,' I said. 'He beat up Noel Cochrane — you can ask Inspector Tirrell about that — and I believe he killed Harriet Williams as well.'

'Here!' said the kneeling constable pain-fully. He was still supporting a large part of the injured man's weight. He had made one attempt to lift Spragg off the spike but the man's protests had left me in no doubt that he would have to be removed to hos-pital with the harrow still attached. 'I know that case,' he said. 'I was on the search team.'

'The man didn't do it,' Daffy said to the policeman. I felt the woman in my arms tense again. Daffy's hand were free now. She rubbed very gently at the raw welts round her wrists. 'This . . . this harpy was the killer,' she said. She was talking partly to me and partly to the bemused youngster. Her words were not easy to make out because she was fizzing with anger. 'They caught me just short of the car. He held me while she tied my wrists and he wasn't being as gentlemanly about it as you are,' she added to me in a furious aside. 'Then he searched me. Not her but him. Some day, if God is good to me, I'll have his balls for that — I'm a respectable, married woman I'll have you know. They took Noel's piece of paper — the bastard still has it on him — and they dumped me in the back of your car and stood looking down at me.'

She returned her attention to the policemen, who were clearly dazed by the rush of unexplained information but doggedly trying to absorb it. The standing policeman had produced his notebook, leaving me to continue hanging onto Miss Otterburn.

Daffy was still spitting out her story. ' "What in God's name do we do with her now?" the man said. The woman said, "She's a damned inconvenient witness. We shouldn't have touched her. We could have blamed our visit on sheer nosiness."

' "We had to see if she had the original of that fax on her," he said. "If she'd hidden it, it might never have turned up. But as it is, she could have produced it. And that would have been the last straw. Now, we can still come off clean. But she'll have to go. How do you fancy a nasty car accident?"

' "I like it, Harry," she said — the bitch!' Daffy exclaimed tearfully. 'Oh, Jesus Christ, the bitch!

'And he said, "If we make it a real good smash, a knock on the head will pass as a result of it."

' "Will you do it?" she asked him.

' "You do it," he said. "You're the expert head-knocker. Do it just as you did to the Williams girl." '

There was a moment of appalled silence.

I must have relaxed my grip on Catherine Otterburn's wrists because her sudden movement caught me unawares and she wrenched herself out of my grasp. 'You bugger!' she yelled. 'You had to open your big trap and now you've dropped me in it!' She snatched up the club from where it lay in the grass. Her fury, I saw, was not focused on Daffy. She made for Spragg who was still crouched in pain over his spike, half supported by one of the constables.

The other officer dropped his pocket-book and managed to catch hold of the pick-handle. He began to recite the usual warning but she was intent on trying to wrestle the club away from him while pouring threats and curses on the agonized Spragg. Her wits seemed to have left her altogether. Suddenly, releasing her grip on the pick-handle, she tried to throw herself on top of

Spragg to drive him down further onto his spike. The kneeling officer had to leave Spragg to support himself. It took the two of them to drag her away, apply handcuffs and lock her into the back of their car.

Daffy and I, meanwhile, had gone to support the unfortunate Spragg. In retrospect I can see a dozen reasons why we might have left him to suffer, but when a fellow human is in great pain it takes a callous spirit to stand back, unmoved. All the same, Daffy spared a hand to retrieve a folded paper from Spragg's breast pocket.

Followed by a flood of muffled invective from inside their car, the two officers returned and took over the duty of supporting the man's weight. Spragg, I saw, had lost enough blood to make a puddle under the harrow and some of it had soaked my knee.

Spragg had enough control of himself to adjust his weight and position until the pain was at its least. Then he managed to speak for the first time, low and huskily but perfectly lucid and intelligible. 'I thought it might come to this,' he said. 'So I kept the evidence. She hit the girl — hit Miss Williams, I mean — with a small cosh, a fisherman's priest we found in the Bothy. She thinks I threw it away as she told me. But, just in case, I picked it up in a polythene bag and hid it.'

Spragg fell silent. I thought that he had

fainted. But he roused again, groaned once and then went on. 'It's under the driver's seat in my car. If it was found, I reckoned that her fingerprints on the brass handle would let me off the hook. I guess there'll be blood and hair on the other end.'

Mike Coutts, I noticed, had produced his pocket tape recorder and was taping what I thought a court could surely accept as admissible evidence in a case of murder.

Twelve

The police took endless statements from us. They were far less zealous about keeping us informed and we depended largely for information on Michael Coutts's published revelations. He had his scoop and he kept it alive and kicking through the disgrace of Hector Tholess and also the criminal trials of Miss Otterburn and her colleagues — trials which resulted in substantial sentences, although the lady was lucky to be convicted only on a reduced charge of manslaughter.

But that was for later. Mike's stories had told the world how we had been more sinned against than sinning and had also gone a long way towards exonerating Noel Cochrane; but we had heard nothing from Noel and our anxiety on his behalf was only relieved when he arrived suddenly on our doorstep one evening to pay an overdue visit to Jove. He looked, I thought, rather worn.

I let the two have a few minutes together before joining Noel outside the wire of the run.

'No sign of rabies,' Noel said. 'And he'll be out of quarantine soon.'

'We're beginning to breathe again. So what happened to you?' I asked sympathetically. 'Are you being prosecuted for blackmail? Charged with theft of documents? Sued for libel?'

He laughed and Jove swept the concrete with his tail. 'None of those,' Noel said.

'What, then? Beth will want all the news when she gets back from Cupar. So spill the beans. Are you in work?'

He sat back on his heels. He was grinning. 'Heads have been rolling at Cook and Simpson,' he said.

'Including yours?'

'Mine was the first to go. But then the more responsible members of the board, the ones who had known nothing about the cover-up, took control and there was a big clearout of staff and resignations on the board. The new chairman decided that somebody had to clear up the mess and that I was the one person who had been right all along. You are now looking, rather incredulously, at the new chief executive.'

I decided that my sympathy had been misplaced. 'And can you clear up the mess?' I asked.

He nodded. 'The old-fashioned way. I'm just throwing money at it until it goes away. There had to be a new share issue, of course, to raise the wind.'

'How on earth did you manage that, in the face of all the scandal?'

'It was oversubscribed,' Noel said complacently. 'Word leaked out at just the critical moment that we had a new golden goose, a vaccination against BSE, the Mad Cow Disease.'

'And have you?'

'I expect so,' said Noel. 'In fact, we'll have to or my head will be on the block again.' He resumed giving Jove biscuits through the wire mesh.

'And I thought that you were the only honest one among the lot of them,' I said admiringly. 'You're as bad as the rest. Come and have a drink, when you can tear yourself away from Jove. I think Daffy wants to tell you all about what she suffered on your behalf.'

'And I want to hear it,' Noel said. 'Give me ten minutes or so.'

He returned his attention to Jove and I left them alone together in the failing light.